PRAISE FOR JACQUIE BIGGAR

"Those of you who love military romance, wounded warrior romance and romantic suspense will love the stories written by this super talented, fabulous author!"

— TAMMY

"Jacquie Biggar had me reading romantic suspense well past my bedtime. The characters are so well written they could walk right off the page!"

— *AVONNA-THE ROMANCE REVIEWS*

"Jacquie Biggar has a wonderful gift for writing hot and extremely likable military men!"

— *JACQUI NELSON*

"This author is an auto-buy for me. Each of her novels including this one is a perfect mix of angst, suspense, humor, and steaminess."

— *STEPHANIE*

VIRTUALLY GONE: A MENDED SOULS NOVEL

High-Tech Crime Solvers - Book 6

JACQUIE BIGGAR

UviArt

Virtually Gone©2020 Jacquie Biggar

This novel is part of *High-Tech Crime Solvers* series, but it can be read as a standalone novel.

Published by Uviart

P.O. Box 3233 Santa Monica CA 90408

Blog: uviart.blogspot.com

Email: uvi.author@gmail.com

First Edition 2020

Printed in the United States of America

 Created with Vellum

For my Family,
If not for your encouragement, I may never have strived to
become a writer.
Now, I can't imagine any occupation that could better allow me
to live my dreams.
Love ya always and all ways,
Jacq

Nothing in life is to be feared, it is only to be understood. Now is the time to understand more, so that we may fear less.

— **MARIE CURIE**

ABOUT HIGH-TECH CRIME SOLVERS

High-Tech Crime Solvers includes:

Virtually Lace by Uvi Poznansky:
Michael Morse, an expert in VR simulation, stumbles on a dead body on the beach. A suspect himself, can Michael stay free for long enough to identify the real culprit?

Virtually Undead by Robert I. Katz:
Neurosurgeon Michael Foreman is drawn into a twisted conspiracy when his best friend is murdered playing a new video game, *Virtually Undead*.

Virtually Harmless by P. D. Workman:
Private consultant Micah Miller's involvement in law enforcement is limited to the composite pictures that she produces with her computer and colored pencils. But every-

thing is turned upside down when she involves herself in the case of an infant found abandoned in the Sweetgrass Hills.

Virtually Dead by Edwin Dasso:

When multiple executives in Vancouver begin disappearing and are then found dead with no signs of trauma, private investigator and former FBI agent Wes Watley is asked by a friend of a friend to investigate.

Virtually Timeless by Casi McLean:

Twins Sydney and Noah Monaco become involved in a conspiracy involving attempted rape, kidnapping, assault and an ancient artifact that isn't supposed to exist.

Virtually Gone by Jacquie Biggar:

When Detective Matthew Roy and reporter Julie Crenshaw are called on to investigate a string of sexual abuse cases, they don't expect Julie to land in the crosshairs of a serial killer.

Virtually Undetectable by Libby Fischer Hellmann:

Fired Bank Manager Rachel Foreman and her mother, renowned investigator Ellie Foreman, track through the lawless corners of the web to find out who is targeting the female CEO of a Fortune 500 company who is accused of murdering a disgruntled former employee.

Virtually Impossible by Barbara Ebel:

Dr. Hook Hookie extrapolates genetic information that informs patients of their hereditary health risks. But he isn't the only one with a use for the high-tech genetic machinery—a villainess with ill purposes stalks the Medical Center.

In addition, the authors compiled this cookbook with recipes cooked by their characters:

Virtually Yummy: Recipes that Inspire

The recipes in this book come from different sources: some of them are family recipes, some were garnered from our travels around the world, and others—inspired by our research, which enables us to write about the adventures of our characters and their culinary feats. But no matter where these recipes come from, we find them not only delicious but also inspiring. We hope you will too.

INTRODUCTION

From USA Today Bestselling Author, Jacquie Biggar, comes a gripping techno-thriller, part of a multi-author series tied together by an interlocking cast of characters, all centered around the fantastic new promise of high technology and the endless possibilities for crime that technology offers, in a world where getting away with murder can be not only plausible, but easy...if you just know how.

Investigative reporter Julie Crenshaw stumbles upon the case of a lifetime--one that could cost her everything

When Julie is called on to investigate a string of sexual abuse cases, she doesn't expect to land in the crosshairs of a serial rapist. Soon she's in a race to find the facts before a killer makes her the headline.

Detective Matthew Roy is frustrated with his inability to

track a rapist terrorizing his city. Added to that, his partner's reporter girlfriend is dogging his every step and won't heed his warnings. Time is ticking with the perpetrator escalating his crime to murder. Matt needs to find the killer soon, or chance losing someone he cares for- the question is, how?

PROLOGUE

Emily Carter shifted the backpack on her shoulder and trudged down the trail toward her parents' house. She hated arguing with Alex, but he didn't understand—no one did.

The wind gusted, whispering through the treetops as the trunks creaked and dropped pinecones like well-aimed bombs. Emily huddled into her hoodie and swiped away her tears. Her emotions were all over the place the last couple of weeks since finding out about...

Her parents were going to be disappointed in her. Between the slipping grades and now this, she'd be lucky if they didn't ship her off to a private school, whether she was sixteen and old enough to make her own decisions or not. Alex was being a jerk. She had a feeling he was going to break up with her soon. She should have known he was only interested in one thing—guys were impossible. He'd been her first real boyfriend. She'd fallen headlong in love and thought he had, too. More fool her.

The lights placed sporadically along the paved trail clicked on, their golden glow trying—and failing—to keep the night at bay. Emily picked up the pace, already anticipating her mother's reaction to her tardiness. If Alex had given her a ride like he'd promised, she wouldn't be walking home in the dark on a chilly autumn night. She'd been battling nausea for the last week or so anyway, the last thing she needed was to catch a cold.

A figure appeared on the path, walking her way and she suddenly became aware of how deserted the trail seemed today. Normally, the well-used Galloping Goose was a hub for students traveling back and forth to school and bikers taking advantage of the handy shortcut to get to work. She kept her head down and hurried along, disquiet replacing her anger with Alex. They met in one of the circles of light and she had the weird sensation she was in a play and didn't know the words. The other person nodded a greeting, but like her, wore a dark hoodie that obscured his features.

A moment later, they separated, each going their own way. Emily heaved a quick sigh to relieve her tension. No wonder her mom told her to quit watching those horror movies—they turned everyday occurrences into nightmares.

When she got home, she'd...

The pain came from nowhere. One minute, Emily was thinking about a hot bath and the next she was on her hands and knees, her head swimming with the force of the blow. A pair of dark sneakers came into view and she had the random thought they were just like the ones her brother wanted for his birthday. A gloved hand grasped her throat and dragged her to her feet.

"You're just like the others," a disembodied voice whispered. "You all think you're too good for me. I've been watching you, Emily. I know what you did."

Scared out of her mind, she tried to get a look at her attacker's face, but he wore a black ski mask. All she could see were glowing eyes and obscene red lips puckered up like a goldfish. But that voice, the lisp—could it be...?

"P... Please, let me go. I won't tell anyone, I promise." She wet herself, the warm liquid between her legs turning her pants cold and clammy. Stupid. She was so stupid to have let herself get into this situation, but she wasn't above begging. "Please, my dad has money. I know he'd give you anything you want. Just let me go."

He pinched her neck harder, his fingers like a vice, and her vision tunneled as she struggled to breathe. "Daddy can't help you get out of this one, little girl. You have everything I want, right now. Time to play." He grabbed her breast through the sweatshirt and gave it a vicious twist at the same time as he bit her bottom lip. "You're going to like what I have—just you wait and see."

Blood flooded her mouth, gagging her even as she fought for enough air to scream. He was going to rape her. She could see it in his feral eyes.

He dragged her off the path and down to the ground. He was rough. Cruel. The pain was overwhelming. And then she knew—she wasn't going to live.

He was going to kill her.

CHAPTER ONE

Detective Matthew Roy crouched near the side of the Galloping Goose Trail and carefully searched the perimeter for evidence. Crime scene techs had cordoned off the location and were photographing the area one quadrant at a time, setting out markers for virtually every bent blade of grass, but he liked to do his own searches. Call him overcautious, but he figured the more eyes on the prize the better the results.

This was the third such assault in a matter of weeks and it was setting the city of Victoria on edge. Notices had gone out not to walk alone, get rid of earbuds while jogging—he hated the damn things, anyway—and stay off the paths after dark whenever possible. For all the good it had done.

He frowned at the dim streetlight creating more shadows than clarity—even with the klieg lights they had set up—and the undergrowth creeping onto the borders of the path. The perfect hunting grounds for his perp. Fifty-five kilometres of paved footpaths with access to a multitude of entry and exit points. The guy was smart. Assuming it was a male,—though Matt knew better than to jump to conclusions—he always used protection which he took with him, kept his head low, wore a dark cap and oversized clothing to mask his size, and the ME was ninety-eight percent certain he shaved all body hair. They hadn't found even one follicle on any of the victims' bodies. Which left Matt batting zero.

"Hey, Detective, got a minute?"

He closed his eyes and drew a deep breath. He liked and admired his partner's new girlfriend, but the last thing he felt like doing was playing nice for the press.

"Can't, Jules, I'm busy." He didn't have to turn his head to see her disapproval, it bore a hole through his shoulders.

"C'mon, Roy. The public have a right to know what's going on. They need to be notified."

That did it. He rose and swiveled on his feet to stomp over and get in her face, heedless of the camera crew waiting in the wings. "What in the h-e-double-l do you think we've been doing?" he roared. Connor had warned him about taking cases like these personally, but dammit, it *was* personal. This young woman had a family somewhere, maybe even a husband and children who would never get to see her or tell her how much they loved her again.

Damn right, it was personal.

Julie jumped backward, her expression frightened before she could wrestle it under control. And now, he felt like an ass. Of course, she was scared. A serial killer had stalked her just as this rapist case was getting under way. Connor had taken lead on the investigation and damn near lost his life.

She gazed at him with worried eyes before turning to her crew and slicing a hand across her throat. "Give us a minute, guys. I'll call you when I'm ready." The group looked at each other, shrugged and gathered their gear, moving to stand beside the VIBS News van. When she returned her attention to Matt, determination overrode the fear. "You want to tell me what has you so riled up?" She raised her hand. "And yes, it's off the record."

No, he did not want to tell the pretty reporter the story of his life, thank you very much. He trusted Julie as much as he did most of the individuals in his life, with the exception of Connor—which was to say, with a bag of salt. He'd found people tended to say what they thought you wanted to hear, not what they actually meant. In his line of work, there was a stark contrast between the two. Which meant he kept to himself, safer that way.

On the other hand, this was Jules. She'd been through some tough times of her own, so he made an effort to tone down his frustration. "I don't like it when I can't keep my city safe," he admitted. He angled sideways so he could keep an eye on the techs. "This guy, it's like he's always one step ahead of us, you know?"

She leaned over the yellow ribbon and patted his too-tense arm. "You'll get him, Matt. I know you will." Then she straightened and donned her investigative reporter face. "Can VIBS get a short statement from you? It doesn't have to give away anything. Just let the public know you're working on it, okay?"

Matt sighed. She was like a Pit bull with a piece of meat. "Yeah, okay. Let's get it over with, I have a case to get back to."

At least she didn't shove her success down his throat. She simply nodded and called her camera crew to get ready, then did something with her hair, twisting the length of it into a loose knot that somehow looked more professional. A microphone was shoved into her hand and then they were live.

"This is Julie Crenshaw with the Vancouver Island Broadcasting System. We are in a wooded area near Harbour Road on the Galloping Goose Trail. Normally a well-used path through the city for cycling and jogging enthusiasts, tonight it became the location of a deadly assault." The camera panned from her earnest face to Matt. "Standing beside me is Detective Matthew Roy. Can you inform the public of what happened here and who you might be searching for?"

Matt gave the usual canned response, aware she'd been hoping for more. "It's too early in the investigation to give out information that could jeopardize the case. A body was located just a few feet away, on the side of the trail, but we won't know whether it is a suspicious death or not until the medical examiner makes his report."

Julie fired back. "Isn't it true that there have been other recent attacks on women using this trail?"

Dammit, she was going to incite a riot if she kept this up. Matt shot her a glare. "I *repeat*, it is too early to determine the cause of death in this case. If there is reason for concern, we will certainly inform the public. Until then, we strongly suggest traveling in pairs and avoiding dark places at night. It's common sense to be careful."

Jules narrowed her eyes at that. "Sound advice, Detective. Would you say the crime rate in Victoria has risen in the past couple of years, and why?"

A tech collected a piece of evidence off the trail and bagged it before carrying it over to the ME crouched near the body of the young woman. She hadn't died easily. He just needed one solid lead, maybe then...

"Detective Roy?"

He jerked and then cursed at getting caught off-guard. "Crime is on the rise everywhere, Miss Crenshaw. I guess you and I have job security, don't we?" He tuned out whatever she said next, his attention on the sealed evidence bag.

Maybe now the hunt could begin.

CHAPTER TWO

J ulie sat at her computer in the madhouse that was VIBS
headquarters and tried to concentrate. Something about
the way Matt had avoided her questions bothered her. Of
course, it was part of the dance journalists and the police did on
a regular basis. Death was always awful, but this seemed...
different. If only she could put her finger on it.

"Hey, Doll-face, what do you have there?" Henderson
invaded her personal bubble to watch the playback of her interview with the detective.

Julie frowned at the cutesy name tag but moved aside so
Ron could see. When she'd first transferred here from Chicago,
the chip on her shoulder had clashed with the laid-back attitude
of the station's lead reporter. It had taken a near-death experience—her second one—to make her realize he was a good guy
under all that persuasive charm.

She eyed the half-eaten donut in his hand and her stomach

grumbled, reminding her she'd been running late this morning and hadn't stopped to eat. And then she remembered *why* she'd been running late and smiled.

Of course, he caught the lustful look in her eyes and attributed it to his food. He shoved the thing in his mouth and swallowed it down. "Sorry, I'd share, but..."

"But you're a pig," she said, humor restored. "And furthermore, it was your turn to buy."

"Hey." He threw his hands in the air, sending grains of sugar scattering. "I did buy. They just didn't make it through the door." His smile was pure mischief and had the desired effect of making her laugh. "That's better," he said. "You were looking grim when I arrived."

She sobered and nodded toward the screen, frozen on a seemingly peaceful bridge with broadleaf maples shading the walkway. "There was another sexual assault," she said. "The victim didn't survive this time."

Ron stared at her for a moment before using his foot to tug an office chair from across the cluttered aisle to her side. He sat, knees butting into hers, and grasped her hands. "Listen, Jules, I know you want to do your job, but after what you've been through, maybe you should give this one a pass."

He was talking about the ABC Killer who'd almost taken her life, of course. But he hadn't, and it was all the more reason she needed to investigate stories like these. If she could save just one woman from the terror she'd felt, or the horror the woman today had gone through, it was up to her to do that. A calling almost. Besides, if it was Ron, he would never quit.

"I can't," she said simply.

He took in her determined expression and leaned back, the chair creaking under his six-four body. "Okay, I get that. But no going it alone this time. You heard Monroe. She'll can your hide if you pull something like that again."

Taylor was her best friend. They'd gone to school together in Chicago. She knew what Julie had been through and was protective. Overly so, at times. Connor, as well. A warmth spread through her chest. He'd been so romantic this morning. With the boys away at her parents' home, they'd been able to properly celebrate their commitment to each other. She was moving on, the death of her husband and child an ache inside instead of the chasm in her heart of the first few months. All the more reason not to take chances.

"I can't let this one go, but I'm willing to accept half the credit if you're interested?" If he agreed, Julie intended to send him to the VIC-PD for an update. It was hard for her to go there now that she was dating a detective. The last thing she wanted was any hint of collusion to ruin either her credibility or a case's chance for a fair trial.

"Nice to hear you two getting along for a change. Did you plan on asking if I could spare Henderson, or were you doing my job again?" Taylor stood behind them, arms crossed and a vexed look in her normally friendly green eyes.

Shoot. Julie and Ron split apart like a couple of naughty school kids. With all the noise in this place, she'd failed to notice the boss's arrival. And that's what Taylor was right now. If she didn't want to lose her job, she had some explaining to do. "I was going to come to your office as soon as I had a firm lead. Ron was just reminding me of your warning about dangerous investigations. I would have talked to you before doing anything, honest." Ron stared at his folded hands resting on his flat stomach. No help there, the big chicken.

Taylor eyed the frozen computer screen. "Is that the murder Detective Roy picked up this morning?"

Of course, she knew. Taylor had connections. Julie nodded. "I can explain—"

"How did you...? Never mind. Did you take a team with you?" Taylor strode between them to restart the video.

"Yes. We didn't get much, though. I was just contemplating my next move when Henderson arrived and ruined my mojo."

At least that got a fleeting smile. Taylor turned back to the screen. "The Galloping Goose again?"

Julie nodded. "Yeah. Third one in as many months. The first two victims won't talk."

"I'll get them to talk," Ron said, apparently done inspecting his belly button.

Julie kicked him behind Taylor's back.

"Cut it out. I swear you'd think you two were related," Taylor muttered, her focus intent on the screen.

Come to think of it, whenever Taylor and Matt were in the same room—which happened now and then since they were her and Connor's best friends—there was a weird vibe in the room. Julie vowed to bring it up with Taylor after work.

When the video ended on the victim's body covered in a white sheet, a pall fell over the three of them until Ron reached over and clicked off the screen.

Taylor turned and leaned against the desk, her skin pale. "Okay. Let's catch this asshole."

CHAPTER THREE

Matt spent the rest of the afternoon filling in a case report and waiting for the ME's phone call. Paperwork was a necessary evil in a police detective's job description. He'd seen too many cases thrown out of court due to an inaccurate paper trail—besides, it helped to ensure he didn't overlook any of the facts. Not that there were many to miss.

Three women; all of differing backgrounds and religions. One, a young woman out to meet friends. The second, an Asian biology student at the University of Victoria. And now, Emily Carter; the youngest at just sixteen. She'd argued with her boyfriend, Alexander Friedman, and run off down the trail, straight into the hands of a heartless killer.

Matt clenched his teeth against the pounding in his skull. Ever since the concussion he'd suffered while chasing a perp a couple of months ago, he'd been getting sudden blinding headaches. He'd laughed when the doctor had suggested avoiding stress. Kind of tough to do in his line of work. He massaged his temples and popped a couple of pain killers, then stood, stretched his back, and crossed the bullpen to refill his coffee cup with the black sludge Esposito insisted on brewing. Matt caught Dan just as he was about to rinse out the pot. "Hold up there, I'll take that."

The wiry cop turned and grinned. "I've finally drawn you over to the dark side, huh?"

Matt scowled as the thicker-than-wallpaper-paste liquid poured into his mug. "It's no wonder you're so damn skinny, this shit'll rot your guts out."

Dan laughed and gave him a well-aimed jab to the kidneys. "What's your excuse then, Roy?"

Matt grunted. "Do that again and your old lady will be having that kid without you." Esposito's wife, Prudence, was due to give birth to their first child any day now, making Dan more haywire than ever.

"Ha, that would leave you to give her comfort and you can forget that idea. My Pru only has eyes for me." Dan winked.

It was true, too. Anyone who saw those two together knew they were a match made in heaven. Didn't mean he couldn't poke fun at his friend though. "Is that why she chose *me* to be the godparent, then? Better watch out, old man, I might just steal her away from you one of these days."

Dan shook his head and carried on with the coffee-making process. "In your dreams, man. In your dreams."

Matt was relieved the exchange, along with the pain pills, had worked to bring his headache down to a dull roar. He decided to take a break from the reports to add the details from the latest crime to his murder board. He'd always been a visual thinker and found using a cork board with photos of the victims, as well as any evidence, on one side and a list of suspects on the other helped him to focus. At the moment, the victims' columns were filling up with information while the suspect pool remained noticeably empty, but he hoped today's attack would turn the tide. If only the ME would call.

Matt turned when Connor entered the quiet conference room, yanking the tie from his neck. "Have I mentioned how much I hate getting called to court?"

Amen to that. Talk about a time suck. Half the cases ended up being dismissed anyway. It was enough to make a guy pull out his hair. Speaking of which... "Did you hear about the assault on the Galloping Goose today?"

Connor threw the paisley tie on the table and took a hesitant sip of Matt's coffee. He grimaced at the taste and set the cup down. "Yeah. It was on the radio. Jules interviewed you?"

"Interrogated, you mean. That woman is like a dog with a bone when she's after a story."

"I don't like it; she's barely recovered from her experience with the ABC Killer. Why can't she be a sports reporter?" Connor shrugged out of his navy-blue suit jacket and undid the top two buttons on his dress shirt. "What do you have so far?"

Matt was still contemplating the benefits of knowing someone who could score cheap hockey tickets. "You should talk to her about that sports thing. She'd get plenty of excitement interviewing athletic types. Never know what kind of perks might come with that sort of gig."

"You're a pig, you know that?" Connor shook his head and stared at the board. "Is that her?"

Sobering, Matt straightened the slightly crooked school photo of the Carter girl lined up next to her crime scene images. "Sixteen-years-old, she had her whole life in front of her." He had to swallow the fury brewing in his chest in order to lay out the facts. "Parents are June and Henry Carter, of the furniture warehouse Carters. They forbade her to date, so she sneaked out to meet her boyfriend. They claim they had no idea. One other child; an older son in university. He wasn't available when I was there today." He took a drink of coffee, barely aware of the bitter taste. "Boyfriend is in the wind. We have an APB out on him. I was thinking of heading over to the coroner's office to try and move them along. Interested in a drive?"

Connor grabbed his jacket, shoved the tie into a pocket and threw it over his shoulder. "Sure, but you know Dr. Robinson doesn't like to be rushed."

"That's why I'm taking you; he likes you better than me," Matt said as they left the station and walked through the parking lot toward his Charger.

"When are you going to let me drive that thing? And he likes you just fine."

Matt slid behind the wheel and started the car. The motor emitted a deep-throated growl, then settle to a contented purr. He waited until Connor was in and belted up to tell him, "Never, you drive like an old woman. It would be an insult to Nelly." He patted the dash lovingly before shifting into gear. "Hang on." He was kidding... sort of. Truthfully, the 5.7 litre engine fed his need for speed and every now and then he took it to the track. But not today.

Twenty minutes later they pulled up in front of the coroner's office. The pathology department was housed in the chilly basement. They entered the building, took an elevator into the bowels of the building, and strode down a long sterile white hall to the forensic pathology wing. A set of double steel doors with windows separated them from the lab. Dr. Robinson glanced up from his inspection of a partially covered body lying on a cold-looking steel table. Thick goggles protected his eyes while a surgical cap hid steely gray hair and a long medical jacket his clothes. He waved them in with a hand gloved up to the elbow.

"Ready?" Connor asked. Before the men entered, they used a menthol balm under their noses and cinnamon gum for their mouths. It helped to cover the stench, but nothing could altogether erase the odor.

Even though they might get some much-needed answers, Matt dragged his feet as he followed his partner into the room that reeked of death.

"ARE YOU SURE?" Matt demanded, staring at the young teen lying on the table with a white sheet covering her from the shoulders down. If not for the pale skin and colorless lips he could almost trick himself into believing she was asleep.

Dr. Robinson removed his glasses and meticulously cleaned the lenses with a soft blue cloth. "I'm afraid so, yes. Barely eight weeks, she might not have even realized she was pregnant yet."

Connor cursed. "Do the parents know?"

Matt let the words wash over him as the medical examiner answered. "I can't comment on that, other than to say not by this office."

"Is there a way to determine who the father is—was?" Matt questioned, rubbing his brow. That damn headache was back.

Robinson nodded, placing his eyeglasses on an eagle-like nose. "A DNA paternity test will give us a definitive answer."

Matt sighed. "Okay, then. Let us know when you have the results; we need them like yesterday. What else do you have for us?"

Connor stepped closer as the doctor turned the victim's head to the side, revealing dark contusions on her neck. "The hyoid bone has been snapped. The same marks are on the other side." He gently turned her head toward Matt and Connor, revealing more blue-black marks like an obscene necklace ringing her frail neck. "Neck compression, or strangulation, can occur with as little as 4.4 pounds of pressure occluding the jugular vein. A man's handshake equals 80 pounds of pressure per square inch." Once more he moved her head, this time so she faced forward. "As you can see here—" he touched a grouping of red dots near the corners of her eyes, "—and here," lifting her lids, "petechiae. Pressure to the carotid artery stopping the flow of blood and oxygen to the brain. Once he got hold of her, she didn't stand a chance."

Matt turned away, gorge rising up his throat. "Was she raped?" he rasped, bending over to clear his head.

"The rape kit will be able to say conclusively, but in my

opinion, yes. There are ligature marks on her wrists, suggesting she was held against her will—"

"No kidding," Matt muttered.

"—and bruising to the thighs and vaginal area," the doc continued. For the first time, he looked uncomfortable. "There are, um, signs suggesting anal force. I've added it to my report."

So, basically, the bastard stole her dignity before he took her life. Matt threw his head back and stared at the ceiling tiles, the lines blurring in front of his moist eyes. He had to get a grip. If only the past hadn't risen like a spectre, reminding him of times he'd sooner forget.

Connor gave him a concerned look before turning to Robinson. "Any good news for us, Doc? Blood under her nails? A stray hair, maybe?"

The ME turned the computer sitting on a pedestal so they could see the screen. "Better. How about saliva found on a bite mark made to her jawline? It produced a DNA match on an unsolved murder from a decade ago."

Matt slowly straightened, the hair on the nape of his neck standing on end. "What case?"

"An eighteen-year-old indigenous girl from Vancouver. She went missing after a dance rehearsal and turned up nine months later in a ditch on the Sea to Sky highway. Autopsy report shows rape and death by strangulation. A strand of dark brown hair was found on her clothing and, at first, discarded as hers until a rookie police officer insisted on an analysis. The DNA test took months to complete and by then it had become a cold case."

He read further down the report. "It says here there were no matches on the National Data Bank's COI list, but they did find three other matches on the CSI list."

Connor frowned. "Three other crime scene investigations from ten years ago? Are you telling me we have a serial killer on our hands, Doc?"

Robinson removed his glasses and carefully placed them in his breast pocket, his gaze somber. "I'm afraid that's exactly what I'm saying, gentlemen."

CHAPTER FOUR

Matt paced the small confines of his apartment, aware of Connor's concerned gaze. They'd come back for a bite to eat, but when he'd opened and closed the refrigerator three times without taking anything out, his friend had pushed him out of the way and offered to cook. The scent of fried onions and garlic should have made him hungry, but all he could think about was Robinson's ominous news.

The shock had receded, leaving pain and hopelessness in its wake—an inky darkness that threatened to swallow him whole.

"Want peppers in your omelet?"

He turned from staring outside, though he couldn't have said what he'd been looking at. "Yeah, sure, whatever you're having. Thanks for taking over. I guess the ME's report threw me more than I'd thought."

Connor cracked four eggs into a blue pyrite bowl and briskly whisked them together. He opened the carton of milk

Matt didn't even remember buying, sniffed the top, then added a dollop to the mixture. Next, he swept the mushrooms and peppers he'd chopped on a cutting board into the bowl and folded them together before dumping the lot into the skillet over the onions.

"You looked as though you'd seen a ghost when Robinson mentioned those cold cases. You want to tell me what that was about?" Connor reached over and dropped the bread into the toaster.

Needing to do something with his hands, Matt poured coffee grounds in the waiting strainer, closed the lid on the tin pot and started the brewing process. He was the only guy he knew who used a percolator. "You're going to find out sooner or later, anyway," he said under his breath.

Turning, he leaned against the counter and crossed his arms. "The indigenous girl was my half-sister, Katrina. I was home when it happened. It destroyed my family."

Connor frowned. "I'm sorry, man, that's rough." He flipped the omelet and turned down the heat before throwing a handful of grated Monterey Jack over the top. "This complicates matters. You'll have to bow out of the investigation."

What? "Not happening. This is my case; you can't take it away from me." Even though O'Rourke could in fact, as a senior officer in their division. The bubbling percolator accentuated his thoughts. "I need to be a part of this, man. Don't make me beg."

Connor shut off the burner under his pan, cut the omelet in half and slid the two pieces on melamine plates just as the toast popped. He dropped them on top of the eggs and carried the dishes to a secondhand bistro table. The chairs didn't look like much, but they supported a man's weight, which was all that mattered as far as Matt was concerned.

"You know the captain would have my head over this," Connor said, lowering himself carefully onto the chair as though he expected the thing to cave under his bulk.

At the moment, Matt almost wished it would. "So, don't tell him," he retorted. "Did I say anything when your girlfriend was in danger? No. Look, my sister died ten years ago—I can handle whatever turns up. Have you ever known me to go off the rails?"

Connor looked up from his plate and raised a brow.

"Never mind, don't answer that," Matt conceded. Noting the coffee was ready, he shut off the stove, carried two mismatched cups and the percolator to the table and set them down before taking a seat. "Just give me a chance. If it gets to me, I'll back off—promise."

Connor let him stew for a while. He poured them each a cup of the dark roast, stirred a heaping spoon of sugar into his and took an appreciative slurp before setting the cup down and easing back on his creaky chair. "Got any ideas where to start? Cold cases become cold for a reason; the evidence trail dries up. We *may* have found a connection to your sister with our vic, but that does us diddly squat in terms of our investigation."

Other than to suggest this guy has been at it for a long time, but Matt understood what he was getting at. "Yeah, actually I do have an idea." He took a bite of his omelet and the flavors exploded in his mouth. "Hey, this is pretty good. Want to get married?" He ducked and chortled as a teaspoon flew past his head. "Watch it, you could take out an eye that way." He picked

24

up the spoon and threw it in the sink. "Julie needs to teach you some manners when you're out."

Connor growled. "Can we *please* get back to the conversation at hand?"

Matt returned to his seat, his shoulders tensing. Much as he professed that he could handle whatever they found, this case was turning into a Pandora's box for him. And once that lid blew off...

"I know someone who does Forensic DNA phenotyping. I'd like to give her a try," Matt suggested.

Connor cocked his head. "Pheno- what?" he asked.

"Phenotyping. She can use the DNA markers found on our victims' bodies to sketch composite images and give us a predictive indicator of gender, eye and hair color, ancestry, and even facial structure. It's like profiling. She helped to solve a case of a missing child last year. You might have seen it on the news? She's in the United States, but works at a private consulting company, so I think it's worth a shot."

"And how much does something like that cost? There's no way the captain will spring for a process that's not even proven."

Matt frowned. "It's new technology, sure, but Micah knows what she's doing. I'll pay for it. I think it's our best bet for finding this guy." *Before he kills someone else.*

Connor rose and took his empty plate to the sink. "Don't get your panties in a knot. I'm just playing devil's advocate. If you trust this Micah, give her a call. We'll go from there."

Not exactly a ringing endorsement, but Matt was willing to try anything that might stop the predator in his city. He fished for his wallet and scrolled through a pile of business cards until he found what he was looking for; Micah Miller, EvPro—Toole County, Montana. It was getting late, maybe he should wait until morning...

She answered on the first ring. "Micah Miller, how can I help you?"

Matt's heart jumped. This was it, he could feel it. "Micah, Matthew Roy here. You may not remember me, but we met at a conference a few years ago."

She came back with a brisk answer. "I remember, the detective from Canada, correct? What can I do for you?"

Straight to the point; he liked her already. "That's right. We have a cold case from ten years ago with the same DNA markers found on a victim we're currently investigating. I understand you can predict age, height, weight, lifestyle. Anything you can give us would be helpful." He braced for her answer.

She released a breath in his ear. "Victim or suspect?"

Matt thought of his sister and his stomach dropped. "Suspect."

Silence other than the scratch of what sounded like a pencil on paper. Matt shrugged at Connor, unsure if he'd said the wrong thing or not. Then came the words he'd hoped to hear.

"I'll do it."

CHAPTER FIVE

After a sleepless night, Matt hit the gym at dawn, determined to face the day with optimism. Too bad his sparring partner didn't get the memo. After getting his bell rung in the ring, he hit the showers and grimaced over the new set of bruises already making an appearance on his ribcage. Maybe he needed to find a new form of exercise—couch potato sounded good about now. Especially since he had to perform a duty dreaded by every cop—notification of death.

Connor was ready when he arrived to pick him up. An intercom at a set of heavy iron gates granted them access to the circular drive and immaculately laid out grounds.

Both men wore uniforms in a show of respect, removing their hats and tucking them under their arms, as they stood at the double front doors of the Carter mansion. Matt raised a brow while they waited. Could the murder be connected to the family's obvious wealth?

The audible click of locks warned them of the upcoming confrontation. Connor straightened, his face grim, and Matt swore under his breath.

A tall, thin blonde stared at them through the narrow gap she'd made in the doorway. "Can I help you, officers?" Her tone was haughty, but trepidation darkened her blue eyes.

"Mrs. Carter?" Connor asked, taking lead and showing his badge. "Is your husband home, ma'am? May we come in for a moment?"

Her gaze flitted from Connor to Matt and back again. "He... he's in his office. What is this about, please?" she asked, her voice rising an octave.

Matt remembered reading the family had moved here from Denmark a few years ago and opened a large furniture chain across the province. The Carters seemed to lead a fairytale life; it was up to him to discover the secrets in their closet. Normally, he enjoyed digging up the dirt on people, but this made his stomach churn.

"I'm sorry, we have some bad news to share. Can you get your husband, Mrs. Carter? It's important." Matt tightened his grip on his hat and fought the urge for a cigarette. He'd quit a year ago, but still craved one now and then when his stress levels ran high.

"Yes, of course," she said, visibly deflating as the severity of the moment took hold. "This way, please." She led them into a sitting room straight out of a style magazine, and with a last nervous glance, hurried to find her husband.

Matt looked around the classically designed room, his attention caught by a group of family photos perched on a wooden mantle over a gas fireplace. He moved closer for a better look, his breath catching on the picture in the center—Emily. The happy young girl with laughing eyes in the photo bore little resemblance to the pale body on the coroner's table.

"Good-looking family," Connor murmured, joining him.

Matt nodded, his throat too tight to talk. He knew from the report the parents were in their late forties with a son three years older than Emily. Damn, he hated this.

"What's going on here?" A man's voice demanded.

Matt and Connor swung as one and stared at the girl's father. Initial moments like these exposed tell-tale reactions that could lead them to the killer. Mr. Carter was shorter than his wife, a bald-headed rooster defending his flock. His cheeks were ruddy, whether it was due to guilt or impending doom, they needed to decide. A recent report stated every 2.5 days a woman or girl was killed in Canada—most by someone they knew and should have been able to trust. So, for the moment, Mr. Carter led their list of suspects.

"Detective Roy and I would like a moment of your time, sir. Take a seat, please." Connor indicated a deep blue velvet love seat in front of the fireplace.

Carter blustered, but subsided onto the sofa, leaving his wife to follow. Matt hid his distaste and took a seat on a chair meant more for decorative purposes than comfort. Connor remained standing, a stalwart presence in the room.

Matt set his hat on the coffee table and sat forward, elbows on knees and hands clasped. "There's no easy way to say this —" he met the growing horror in Mrs. Carter's eyes, his heart hurting, "your daughter was murdered last night on the

29

Galloping Goose Trail. We believe she was on her way home at the time."

The poised woman who'd met them at the door disappeared in a swelling tide of despair. She vigorously shook her head, her hand reaching out to clasp her husband's. "No, you've made a mistake. Emily was home last night. I brought her home from school myself. It's not possible." She broke down then, great flowing tears washing away the carefully applied makeup, leaving a pale facsimile of the woman behind.

"Can you specify the last time you saw your daughter, Mrs. Carter? Was she... upset?"

"How do you know it's our child?" Carter asked, his voice gruff with pent-up emotion. "It could be anyone's."

Desperate parents in denial. Matt wished he could give them the news they wanted to hear. "The ME—medical examiner—made a positive ID based on dental records. She didn't suffer for long," he added, grimacing inwardly at the mother's heart-wrenching sobs. Like he said, this sucked.

"Mr. Carter, is your son home today?" Connor offered a box of tissues to the couple.

Carter glanced at him with suspicious red eyes. "Why? What do you want with our boy?" Then he rose and glared at them. "Are you suggesting Emily's brother did this?" he screeched, spittle flying from thick lips. "Get out. Leave now and don't come back unless you have a warrant. Do you hear me? Get. Out!"

Left with no other choice, Matt rose. He hated to leave the girl's mother without at least trying to help. He pushed his card into her clenched hand. "If you think of anything, or just need to talk, please don't hesitate to call. We have counsellors on staff, or you can reach me at that number anytime. We won't stop until we catch whoever murdered your daughter, Mrs. Carter. I promise, okay?"

She made no sign that she heard him, but her grip tightened on his card. It was the best he could do. They strode to the door, conscious of Carter's angry presence dogging their tracks.

Connor turned to face him before they left. "If there's something you're not telling us, it would be in your best interests to come forward," he said. "We're on the same side."

Carter's gaze turned hard. "And what side is that, Detective? I read the stories. I know how often the police blame undeserving victims of your system in order to make their arrests, so they come off looking the heroes. You will not be doing that to my family. Not while I'm alive to stop you." He slammed the door in their faces and in a final act, reengaged the locks.

"So," Matt said. "That went well."

CHAPTER SIX

J ulie sipped a refreshing cooler and tapped her toes to the jazz band playing on stage at the front of the bar. It was two days late, but Taylor had asked if she was interested in hearing her brother's group and she'd jumped at the chance.

It was a Sunday evening, so the room wasn't crowded, which suited her just fine. The last few days had been a crazy round of chasing stories and working on the Galloping Goose rapist investigation. She needed a break.

She'd talked to Dustin and Freddy briefly this morning before church and they'd promised to lay a flower for her on their father's grave. Tomorrow, they were going to the zoo. At least they were having a good time with their grandparents back home in Chicago.

"Oh, good, the drinks arrived." Taylor slid onto her barstool after a trip to the ladies' room. "What do you think of Norman's band? They're good, right?" Pride shone from her shiny blue eyes. Ash-blond hair fell in a sweep over her shoulder, giving the tough television producer a softer, more vulnerable appeal.

Julie glanced at the band again, watching appreciatively as the only blond guy in the group performed a guitar solo. "Is that him?" she asked and smiled at Taylor's enthusiastic nod. "They're amazing—really."

"This is only their second gig. He was a nervous wreck." Taylor laughed.

"Well, he didn't need to worry. The crowd loves them."

Connor was joining them later. Maybe she could convince him to dance. He wasn't big on socializing but did it for her. Another sign he cared. Her heart fluttered.

"What are you thinking about... oh, your cop. You have it bad, don't you?" Taylor teased, then squeezed her wrist. "You deserve it, hon."

Julie wanted to believe her, but between the death of her husband and almost getting murdered by a man she thought she could trust, she was scared to reach for happiness. "We're taking it slow, we both have baggage."

"Honey, we all do." Taylor leaned closer. "Life is short, you need to reach out and grab it with both hands." She sat back and lifted her drink to her lips. "Or regret that you let it slip away."

Julie's reporter instincts kicked into gear. That speech seemed self-directed. They'd been friends for a long time, but Taylor had never been one for confidences. Was she naturally reticent or was there more to the story?

"Is something wrong, Taylor? You've seemed stressed the last while. Is there anything I can do?"

She owed her friend for giving her the opportunity to start a new life here in Victoria. It had enabled her little family to move on from their tragic past, though it helped they had Mike's spirit watching over them. As usual, thoughts of her late husband sent a warm glow through her body—almost as though she was wrapped in his loving arms again. Another reason to take her new relationship with Connor slow; Mike was still a large part of her life. She wasn't ready to let him go.

Taylor frowned into her drink. "A friend from Vancouver called earlier today. Apparently, her executive husband, Michael Saleen, went missing a few days ago and she's out of her mind with worry." She met Julie's gaze; her mouth grim. "The police are writing it off as a middle-aged crisis. They think he's holed up with some woman having an affair, but Sherry says no way, he'd never do that, and I tend to agree with her."

"That's awful," Julie said. "Isn't he the guy we went to school with? The one with the crazy GPA?" She was surprised the police would take that stance. Unless they had reason to believe... "He was a nice boy. Do you want me to look into it for you? I have a few contacts with the VPD and city hall, maybe they could shed a light on their findings."

Taylor looked relieved. "Could you? That's the trouble with taking a management position, my street cred is gone." She tried to smile but it fell flat. "Sherry called in a retired FBI Agent, now a personal security consultant, to see if he could find anything. Wes Watley, have you heard of him?"

No, but Julie had a feeling that was about to change. "I'll leave Ron to interview the neighborhood where our victim's family lives while I take a quick trip over to the mainland. We can interview the parents together in a day or two—give them time to come to grips with the loss of their daughter."

"I appreciate this," Taylor said, turning to watch her brother finish his set. "I don't know what I'd do if someone came after my family." She lifted her glass to catch the eye of a passing server. "Enough of this depressing talk, how are your kids liking their time with the grandparents?"

Julie nodded to the server's two finger enquiry on their refills and smiled at her friend. "They're having a blast—especially since you gave them each a hundred bucks to spend. You shouldn't have, they're spoiled enough."

Taylor shrugged, "You shouldn't have made me their godmother then. That's what we do." She glanced toward the door and her eyes widened. "Oh, oh. You're about to get busted."

Julie twisted around and that fluttery attraction thing started again. Connor and Matthew stood in the doorway, searching the crowd until they found her. Connor lifted his hand in a salute and the men started across the room, drawing the eye of every female in the place. And why not? They were both dressed in dark jeans and button-down shirts, blue for Connor, white for Matt, and walked like they owned the floor. It was sexy, no two ways about it.

"Hey," he said, giving her shoulder a warm squeeze, "mind if we join you?"

Taylor had that enigmatic look again, but she waved them to a chair. "Only if you're buying," she quipped.

Matt took the seat to her right and grinned. "A lady after my own heart. What are you having?"

She shot him a glance beneath her lashes. "Nothing that you can handle. Rye and coke—double."

He raised his brows. "Tough day?"

She raised her chin. "You could say that."

"Me, too," he answered. "I'll have what she's having." He smiled up at the cute server as she set down the glass. "Connor?"

"Coffee—black. Someone had better stay sober to drive these delinquents' home," he said, mouth lifting in that adorable quirk.

Julie grinned but her attention was caught by the bickering going on between their table mates. She wondered how long it was going to take for the fireworks to start.

MATT TOOK another drink of his rye and coke and felt the day's tension slowly fade away. Ten years on the job and it never got easier notifying family members of a loss. And it was even worse when it came to kids.

He wouldn't have pictured this dark lounge as a hangout for reporters, but it had its charm. The tables were far enough apart to give a sense of intimacy while still being part of the crowd enjoying the band on stage. They weren't half bad, he mused. Not his normal taste in music, which ran more toward old school rock and roll, but they knew how to carry a tune. He smiled at Connor's awkward dance moves; the boy had no rhythm. Damn impressive that Julie had managed to drag him onto the dance floor, actually. But then again, when you're smitten, you'll do things you never thought you'd do.

The table jiggled under his arm and drew his attention to the woman who'd been studiously ignoring him for most of the evening. Taylor Monroe came off as a hardass, but there were moments, like now, as she watched her friend dance, that he sensed a kindred spirit. He was also wary of getting hurt, and held himself emotionally aloof because of it. It was a lonely way to live.

"So... what's a nice woman like you doing in a dive like this?" *Lame, Roy, really lame.*

Taylor quit clinking the melting ice in her still-full glass to stare at him with narrowed eyes. "Does that line ever work for you, Detective?"

Now that he felt like a bug about to get squished under her heel— "Got your attention, didn't I?" His lips quirked. "Who's the guy you keep staring at on the stage, a boyfriend?"

"Brother," she replied. "Younger by two years, accountant by trade, single, never been in trouble with the law—at least so far as I know—anything else?"

Matt held up his hands. "Whoa, not every question I ask is professional. Maybe I was just making small talk with a beautiful woman while our friends tear up the dance floor, okay?"

Her forehead furrowed as though she had a headache coming on—he could relate. She released a long sigh. "Sorry. I'm not used to this..." she waved her hand between them, "casual encounter thing. Work has ruled my life for so long, I've forgotten how to act normal, I guess."

Again, he could relate.

Maybe it was time they both made some changes. He stood and held out his hand. "Someone once told me, 'it's never too late to become the man you want to be.' Tonight, I want to channel my inner Fred Astaire." He grinned. "Join me?"

She hesitated so long, he thought he'd be dancing with himself, but then she gave a determined nod and slid off her stool. "Okay, Fred, show me what you've got."

Now probably wasn't a good time to tell her he had two left feet.

The lounge had filled since he'd arrived, and it took some snaking to make their way to the polished wood floor in front of the stage. Couples twirled and swayed to the song the four band members performed, their shuffling steps creating an accompanying beat to the music. The overhead lights were angled toward the stage, leaving the dancers in a more intimate setting.

Taylor pulled back on his arm, stopping them on the edge of the floor. "It's busier than I expected, maybe we should sit this one out."

Matt turned from his surveillance of the dancers to see her furrowed brow again. That sealed the deal, they both needed to let their hair down and do something out of character for a change. "No way, I'm not fighting my way through that bunch again. Your brother has a serious fanbase," he said, drawing her reluctantly forward. "Come on, it won't hurt too bad." He hoped.

It was awkward at first; she didn't seem to know where to put her hands any more than he did. He took the fingers he held and placed them on his shoulder—her touch soft, feminine— then set his on her slim waist. "Ready?"

She gave a hesitant nod. "As I'll ever be."

The first few steps were a mishmash of glides and shuffles and bumping into other couples, but they didn't give up and soon were doing a fair imitation of actual dance steps.

"See, I told you we could do it," Matt said, gazing into her upturned face. She really was quite lovely with her mesmerizing blue eyes and blond hair. She grinned and it lit up those eyes. He wanted to keep making her smile, take away some of the stress he'd sensed earlier. "Ready for a dip?"

"Don't you dare," she cried, laughing. "You'll break your back—and mine."

"Huh," he teased. "That sounds like a challenge to me."

"Matt..." she warned, then something over his shoulder took her attention.

He slowed, picking up on her tension. "What's—"

Connor and Julie appeared at their side, expressions grim. "Gotta go, we have another one."

Matt cursed. "Same MO?"

Connor didn't answer, his gaze flicking to Taylor.

Oh, yeah, he'd been flirting with a news journalist. Matt released his hold on her and took a step back. "Duty calls. Are you going to be okay to get home?" He didn't like the thought of her in a dark parking lot, especially with a killer on the loose.

She ignored his question to lob one of her own. "Is this about the Galloping Goose attacks?" She leaned in, her expression fierce. "I'm coming."

"Me, too," Julie announced. "This is my story."

"Like hell," Matt and Connor said in unison. The couples nearby startled. Matt frowned and dragged Taylor to a semi-secluded area near the corner of the stage, aware of her brother's concerned stare following them. At least she wasn't alone.

"You can't go—"

"You can't stop—"

They glared at each other. Matt sighed, well aware if he couldn't convince her to back down, she'd just follow them to the location. "Look, I know you need your story, but you have to let me do my job first. The more people on scene, the more the evidence is destroyed. It doesn't matter how careful you are." He could see the reluctant acknowledgement in her expression and pressed home his point. "It's our duty to protect the public, too, Taylor. Let us do our job."

She frowned and looked past him at the unaware crowd laughing and drinking, having a good time. Any one of them could be next if he didn't get this guy off the streets.

"Fine," she said. "Go. But you better keep us in the loop. I want my story, Detective."

He nodded, relieved. Hopefully, it would be a short story with the criminal behind bars.

CHAPTER SEVEN

Glen Lake reflected the moon's glow, dancing with ghostly fingers of fog that coiled through the tall fir trees circling the water. The body was a dark mound on the grass near the public restroom, hand splayed out like a silent cry for help.

Matt clenched his fists. "Where the hell were the extra patrols I ordered?"

"Last time I checked, nobody made you captain yet, Roy. We're already spread thin with these protests and lack of funding. We're doing the best we can," D'Costa said, his face grim as he squatted near the woman's head. "Second homicide in a month—you're racking them up, Detective. Figure this one links to the rapist case?"

"You know what they say about assumptions, right?" Connor hiked up the sidewalk from the beach where he'd been talking to investigators. "Let's stick with the facts and leave the guessing to the press." He nodded to a couple of dark figures stringing yellow tape around the playground. "Mind giving those two a hand setting up a perimeter?"

D'Costa rose. "Yeah, sure. Did anyone hear anything?"

"Esposito is doing a door-to-door as we speak."

The ME's van pulled into the parking lot.

"Maybe now we can get some answers." Connor met Matt's gaze as D'Costa headed across the loamy grass. "Something you want to talk about?"

Matt frowned. "This is our fault. If we were doing our job, she'd be alive." He scrubbed the back of his neck. "It's frustrating as hell."

Connor nodded. "I get it, really I do. But going off on our guys isn't going to solve anything. We're on the same side, don't forget that."

Matt thrust his hands in his pockets and watched his friend stride up the walk to meet the M.E. If he didn't get control of his temper, his days of working this investigation were numbered. He couldn't stand the thought of stepping back—not now that they were finally getting somewhere. Ten long years his family had been without answers in his sister's murder—it was time to catch her killer.

"Detective Roy, what have you got for me?" Doctor Robinson asked, squinting at him through plain, black-rimmed bifocals.

"Hey, Doc, thanks for coming out. Vic is Caucasian, mid-twenties, no ID that we could find. Looks as though he chased her through the sand and up to here." Matt pointed toward the beach. "We found a shoe matching the one on her foot down near the dock."

Robinson glanced at the twinkling lights from the houses rimming the lake. "Out for an after-dinner walk, perhaps?" He nodded toward faint indentations in the grass. "Too deep for her. You'll want to have your CSIs do a depth and size analysis. Might help with your profile." With that, he snapped on a pair of white plastic booties and gloves for his hands, then made his way carefully over to the decedent's half-naked body. "Anyone touch her?" he asked, creating an incision under the ribcage to carefully insert a thermometer into the abdominal cavity.

"No, we were waiting for you." Connor crouched near the foot depressions and set an orange marker up before snapping some photos. "We have the perimeter cordoned off."

"Good, good. You wouldn't believe how much evidence gets destroyed by compromised crime scenes." Removing a kit from his bag, Robinson swabbed under the nails, then placed plastic bags on her hands and zip ties to wrap around the wrists. Next, he shone a penlight over her face and gently moved aside dark brown hair to show a contusion still wet with congealing blood on her scalp. "May have been caused by a blunt instrument like a bottle. I'll take samples for now and x-rays once we get back. Tell your men to keep their eyes out for any fist-sized weapons."

A glance down the length of her body lowered his brows. "Her clothes are torn below the waist." He looked at Matt and Connor with grave eyes. "I'd like to do a preliminary rape kit on her. Can you get your techs to set up a privacy tent, please? This young lady has been through enough indignities."

43

"Of course," Connor said, turning toward the beach. "Right away."

After he was gone, Matt rocked back on his heels, strangely reluctant to voice the question they all wanted answered. "Do you think it was the same guy, Doc?"

Robinson pushed his glasses up his nose and stared at the water for a moment. "I can't say for certain," he said at last. "But the ligature marks around the neck look the same. I'll be able to tell more after we do a thorough inspection."

"Can you give us an approximate time of death?"

"I'd say no more than one-to-two hours. The internal temperature is near normal, lividity is unfixed and consistent with her position, and there's only slight rigidity in her jaw and fingers."

Matt's pulse skipped a beat. If that was true, the perp could be nearby depending on his mode of transport. They could have driven right past him on their way to the scene. Or maybe he lived in the area and was literally under their noses this very minute. Normally, pursuing evidence, connecting the dots, sleuthing, made the job interesting. But this time, he would give anything to skip straight to the arrest.

Connor arrived with a couple of white garmented CSIs carrying a portable tent and better lighting. "Up for a drive? Esposito caught a lead a few blocks from here. Someone heard a noise in their garage and scared off an intruder."

"What are we waiting for?" Anticipation buzzing under his skin, Matt led the way to the parking lot and waited impatiently for Connor to unlock his car. Every second counted. He could almost feel the bastard laughing at them and it pissed him off.

"This is bullshit," he muttered as Connor backed up and headed up the hill leading from the lake. "He's toying with us. Ten years nothing—that we know of—now, all of a sudden, he's attacked four women in the space of three months. Why here? And what's with the escalation? It's frustrating the hell out of me."

"You don't say." Connor turned down the alley and slowed. "You're leading with your emotions, buddy. Calm down and think like a cop. The evidence will uncover our suspect, we just have to pay attention to the clues and not go off half-cocked."

Easy for him to say, he hadn't lost his sister to a killer.

"I'm trying, man, but I can't help thinking we're missing some..."

A dark figure burst into the alley, highlighted for a second by their headlights before he dodged into the bushes on the other side. Connor slammed on the brakes even as Matt opened his door and jumped from the car, drawing his weapon. Esposito ran into view and waved them forward, directing the chase. The three detectives dashed into the shadows in pursuit.

Matt's heart thundered, his back plastered to the rough wooden wall of a carport. Connor had split left, Esposito right, as they circled the edge of the fenced backyard leading up to a dark older home. Esposito shouted a warning just as a dog erupted into frantic barking in the next yard. Matt jerked backward and cursed as a board swung past his head.

"Stop, this is the police. Put your hands up," he shouted after the running figure. He gave chase, aware of Connor and Esposito scurrying to catch up. The guy was fast—and agile.

Matt huffed and cursed as he fell further and further behind. If he didn't catch a break soon, the asshole would disappear.

Just then, a car turned into the alley from the opposite end and highlighted the fleeing man in its lights. Instead of slowing, the two raced toward each other in a macabre game of chicken. Matt yelled, an ugly certainty growing in his chest. Sure enough, a moment later the car slammed to a stop and the guy crawled in on the passenger side. The driver hit his brights, blinding Matt, and reversed at high speed back the way he had come before burning a shit-hook and roaring off into the night.

Matt stood there, gripping his gun and breathing hard. He'd come so close to crossing a line tonight and pulling the trigger. It scared him worse than losing the suspect. Connor was right, he needed to take a step back. Before this case cost him his career.

CHAPTER EIGHT

J ulie paced her bedroom like a twitchy cat, stopping to stare out the window at the empty street, then across to her silent cellphone on the dresser. Connor had been gone for hours without word—it was driving her mad.

The house was too quiet without her boys. Usually, she'd hear Dustin tossing and turning, and Freddy's light snores, but tonight there was only silence. It unnerved her. Ever since she'd been kidnapped by the ABC Killer, the smallest things made her jumpy. She used her job as a journalist to combat the fear, to do what she could to protect victims like her. And yet, another rapist was loose in their city.

She shivered and left her room to double-check the locks.

There'd been two rapes near the university a couple of months ago. The women had escaped with their lives but were brutally beaten and robbed at knifepoint. Then there was the young girl last week, barely old enough to drive, killed just minutes from her home. The police were assuring the public they had no reason to be alarmed, whereas Julie disagreed. Maybe if those targets had been warned of the danger, they would have stood a better chance of avoiding his trap. If there was one takeaway she'd learned from her own experience, it was that psychopaths were in it for the thrill of the chase. They got off on terrifying their victims. The only answer was to take away their power.

Which was why she was up pacing instead of getting some much-needed sleep. Connor was keeping things from her and she didn't like it. Either there was trust in their relationship, or it couldn't continue. She didn't expect him to divulge details of the investigation, but at the same time, she wasn't just any reporter, either. He knew how personal cases like this were for her—she'd defied death and now it had become her calling to help others going through the same thing. Beating back the monsters one story at a time.

She turned from the locked front door and stopped in front of Mike's photo hanging in the hall. Her husband's green eyes stared at her with a perpetual smile. He had been the light in their relationship. Able to drag a laugh out of her even in her grumpiest days, and was a wonderful father to the boys—their baby girl would have loved him, too, if not for the accident that took their lives. Julie liked to think father and daughter were together now, watching over their family. He'd certainly been there for her when that madman had chased her through the woods a few months ago. He'd given her the strength to hold on until help could arrive.

"I miss you so much," she murmured, her finger tracing the

glass. "I think you'd like Connor... he's a good man." Warmth filled her chest and Mike's eyes seemed to glow with tenderness and a sad acceptance. He would always be her first love, the gangly teen who'd stolen her heart and given her two beautiful sons, but he was gone and life moved on. She hadn't expected to fall for another man. For a long time, she'd put her growing feelings down to loneliness, but Connor had impacted her life too much to be ignored. He could be arrogant at times, and overprotective, but he was also sweet and incredibly patient with Dustin and Freddy. She was happy for perhaps the first time since the accident that took her husband and unborn daughter. Was it wrong to wonder when the other shoe would drop?

The phone rang in the bedroom and she hurried down the hall, expecting it to be Connor. Instead, Taylor's number showed up on the display.

"Hi, what are you doing still awake?" Julie asked, sitting on the edge of her bed and tucking bare toes into a plush throw rug she'd grabbed from a bargain bin.

"Sorry to call so late," Taylor said in her no-nonsense voice. "I managed to book you onto a seaplane to Vancouver tomorrow morning. Can you make it?"

Julie blinked. *What...?* Oh, yeah, the private security consultant she was supposed to meet. With everything else that happened tonight, it had slipped her mind.

"Tomorrow is fine. The kids come home this weekend, so I'd just as soon get it over with. What was his name, again?"

"Watley. Wes Watley. Ex-FBI and Army CID Officer. He knows his stuff. Hopefully, you can bounce ideas off each other and come up with a solid lead. You never know, maybe he can even suggest something to catch our rapist."

Privately, Julie was more cynical on that score. She'd met FBI types before and found them to be close-mouthed, but maybe this would be different. A little quid pro quo. "Where do we meet?" she asked, turning as the front door opened and closed.

"He's coming into YVR at nine. By the time he gets through customs you should be able to catch him near the baggage claims." Taylor paused. "Sherry is a mess over this. Anything you can do to help..."

Julie wandered to the dim hallway in time to catch Connor rubbing a tired hand over his neck, the streetlight from outside turning his hair to burnished copper. He stopped when he noticed her and raised his brow. Her pulse scattered.

"Of course," she murmured. "Can you send me a recent photo of Mr. Watley, so I know who I'm looking for?" If not, she planned to do an online search for his company, his bio should be there.

"You'll have it by morning," Taylor assured her. "It shouldn't take more than a couple of days. An introduction to your contacts with the VPD should set him on the right track. Thanks, Julie."

"No problem. See you when I get back." Julie ended the call and strode into Connor's welcoming embrace. His chest was warm and comforting, the arms around her waist strong, yet gentle. He nuzzled the top of her head and she leaned back to look at his face. "Hi," she said softly, concerned by the dullness in his normally expressive eyes. "Long night?"

"You could say that," he agreed, bending to steal a kiss. "I thought I was dreaming when I walked in. That shirt never looked half as good on me."

She glanced down, then bit her bottom lip. Their seamed bodies from the waist down betrayed what he thought of her nightwear choice. Her bare legs tingled, suddenly sensitized to the scrape of jeans and the muscular length of his thighs.

Breathless, she took a step back, not yet ready to let go of her reporter's curiosity. "Was it the rapist?" Objectively, she realized all of their callouts wouldn't be over one case, but something told her that's exactly what happened tonight. The hunter had claimed another victim.

Connor sighed and pocketed the keys she'd given him a month ago. "We won't know for sure until the autopsy is done, but yeah, we think it's the same guy." His lips tightened into a faint grimace as he toed off his shoes. "We just about had him until the bugger used a two-by-four to try and play baseball with Matt's skull."

Julie gasped. "Oh, no. Is he hurt?" She knew their job was dangerous, but this highlighted the risks they took every time they went on a call.

Connor shook his head and brushed by her to stride down the hall toward the single bathroom in the old house. "Nah, he got lucky this time. The perp had an accomplice, though. We weren't expecting that. Drove right up and plucked him out of our hands sweet as a momma with her baby." He glanced back and lowered his voice. "I need a shower. You joining me?"

Much as Julie wanted to hear more of the story, a deeper need to erase the distance between them grew. Slowly, deliberately, she grabbed the hem of his worn shirt where it ended at the tops of her thighs and lifted it over her head before letting the material drift to the floor. "I'm ready. What are you waiting for?" She was never so brazen, but it was thrilling to see his fatigue disappear as desire took over.

The hair on her arms and nape rose with his hot stare. She shivered, light-headed, as he reached her in two strides and pushed her back against the wall. He devoured her, there was no other word for it, sending her pulse skittering every which way. Their tongues twisted and tangled. His big, capable hands grasped her butt, lifted, and her legs automatically wrapped around his waist, sealing them together. His mouth moved down her neck, suckling and nipping until her head spun. She whimpered and burrowed her fingers into his hair, urging his lips to hers. The very air around them seemed to turn dark and sultry with promise. Eyes heavy-lidded, jaw taut, Connor turned with her in his arms and carried her into the shower. All thoughts of tomorrow's trip or tonight's uneasiness faded beneath an onslaught of steamy passion.

Time enough for talk later.

CHAPTER NINE

Matt needed sleep, but he needed a break in the case more, so he went back to the precinct and his murder board. He had to be satisfied with Doctor Robinson's promise to add the new Jane Doe to the top of his priority list. The man was thorough and wouldn't appreciate getting pressure from them on how to do his job.

The bullpen was quiet. A couple of officers wrote reports while cleaning staff pushed mops and wiped down desks; other than that the offices were dark. This was his favorite time to be in the station. The silence let his mind wander and nerves settle. He should probably get busy on his own report, but first he wanted to cement the night's events on his pegboard. In the morning, he planned on meeting with a sketch artist to get down a description of the suspect—though he'd been too busy protecting his noggin to get a good look at the creep.

He flicked the switch and listened to the lights hum to life in the small boardroom. His gaze went to the notes he'd taped to the easel, starting with the first victim and persons of interest in each incident. Opening the file he'd brought with him, he withdrew the pictures from tonight's crime scene and added them to the ever-widening circle he'd created. A pattern was forming. With the exception of the Carter girl, the perp focused on women in their early twenties with dark hair and slim builds. He took advantage of location—choosing areas with little, or no, lighting—and time of day. Planning his attacks between six and eight in the evening, when people were out walking and suspicion would be low.

Gina Davis, the first victim, had been heading home after an evening biology class at the university. She'd taken two different buses before getting off five blocks from home. She'd stopped in at the local grocery store, picked up a few essentials, paid with her debit card, and exited onto the Galloping Goose Trail which ran right past her street. Security cameras at the store put the time at seven thirty-five p.m. Interviews with staff stated she was a regular, always pleasant and friendly. Roommate notified police when Davis failed to arrive home or answer her cellphone. After receiving a statement, parents, family, and friends were informed and questioned. A search of the area was underway, hampered by the hour, rain, and rugged terrain. Three hours later, Davis was found unconscious, bound, beaten and gagged, several feet into the underbrush. She'd been raped and left for dead, but by some miracle, survived the attack. The severity of the assault left her with a temporary amnesia and there was very little she could divulge to help them catch the perpetrator.

The second incident happened a month to the day later. Teresa Kellerman planned to meet a group of friends at a nearby lounge for drinks after their shift at the hospital. Teresa was an avid biker and used the Galloping Goose Trail to escape the heavy downtown traffic. Her bright yellow bike was found tossed into a ditch by a passerby. He noticed what looked like dried blood on the crossbar and immediately began a search of the area. A half a kilometre away, he spotted Kellerman's naked body floating in the Gorge Waterway and called 911 for help. She was taken to emergency and remained in an induced coma for three days. When she came out of it, she refused to talk—her face a swollen mass of cuts and bruises. Teresa had been brutally raped, and as with the other cases, they had little evidence to go by.

Matt sat on the table and rubbed the back of his neck. Two young women with their whole lives in front of them until a monster ripped the rug from beneath their feet. It would be months, maybe even years, before they could function normally again, build relationships, have families of their own. He'd seen it happen from the other end of the spectrum.

Families also paid a steep price at the loss of a loved one —guilt.

When Katrina was murdered his parents blamed themselves. Hell, he did, too. He'd been seventeen when she went missing—a punk kid who thought he knew everything, but really knew nothing at all. Kat may have been his older half-sister, but she always had time for him—she listened when no one else did. And it was his fault she died. If he'd done as his mother asked and driven to the dance studio to pick Kat up like he was supposed to, maybe she'd still be alive. Instead, he'd taken his sweet-assed time chatting with a girl—he couldn't even remember her name now—and it cost his sister her life. After she was gone, their house became an empty shell. The laughter leached out of the walls and the sun refused to enter through the windows. It was as though Katrina took their souls with her when she left. Six months later, his parents separated, and Matt fell into a bottle to ease the pain. The police came by now and then to update them on the investigation, but he could see in their eyes they weren't invested in the case. After all, another indigenous woman going missing barely made the morning news. And then a body was found on the Sea-to-Sky highway and Matt had known—Katrina had been found.

"Long night." Esposito said from the doorway, startling Matt. "Just finished writing up my report."

Matt tapped his skull. "Thanks for the heads-up earlier, that board came out of nowhere."

Esposito wandered into the room, his gaze on the photos. "I hate it when the bad guy wins," he murmured.

Fists clenching, Matt rose. "He won't win the next time."

Dan's brow rose. "You know something I don't?"

Matt expelled a deep breath and pointed to the photos of the victims. "Because they're going to help us catch him. We just need to read the signs."

Dan scratched his head. "Well, I don't know about any of that hocus-pocus stuff, but there was a message on your desk from a... Micah Miller? She said it's important and to call her back as soon as possible."

Matt's pulse leapt. He needed a miracle and Micah might

be the one to give it to him. "That was quick." He pulled his cell from his pocket. Sure enough, he'd missed a call. "I need to get this, do you mind?"

"Nah." Dan patted his arm and headed for the door. "Pru wants me to pick up ice cream to go with her pickles. Pregnant women sure have strange cravings. Night, man."

Matt was already dialing and barely registered his friend's words or the closing door.

"Hello?" Micah answered.

"Ms. Miller? It's Matthew Roy, I understand you might have some information for me?" His palms grew sweaty and he transferred the phone to speaker before setting it on the table.

"You understand this is subjective, correct? I can give my best analysis, but that's all it is—it won't stand up in court."

"I'm aware of the ethical and moral issues, yes. Tell me what you've got." He sat down and opened his notepad, his heart pounding.

"Genetic testing is already in use to determine patients who may develop certain types of cancers or a wide variety of other diseases. FDP, or Forensic DNA Phenotyping, takes that technology to the next level and can predictably identify outstanding characteristics such as the gender of a person with one hundred percent accuracy."

She cleared her throat. "We can also predict with nearly seventy percent accuracy physical characteristics such as age, skin, hair, and eye color. We've made great progress in identifying such features as ethnicity, dominant hand usage, height, male pattern baldness, face morphology and more.

"I mention this so that you will understand how I came to

create my profile for your suspect. You're looking for a male, Detective. Age range; mid-to-late forties, Caucasian, with thin, dark hair—possibly bald on crown. Brown or hazel eyes, right-handed and approximately six feet tall." She hesitated, then added, "I can send you a sketch if it would help."

This was more than Matt could have hoped for—finally, a solid lead. "I'd appreciate it, Micah. You've helped tremendously. I don't know how to repay you."

A soft, sad sigh came down the line. "Just catch him," she whispered.

Damn right. He was going to do everything he could to make that request a reality.

CHAPTER TEN

Julie stared out the window as the cab skated in and out of the busy Vancouver traffic. Skyscrapers towered overhead, vying with a watery blue sky to shed light on the streets far below. Hydrangeas in a rainbow ribbon of pink, blue, and purple fought for space with heather, lavender and rhododendrons under fiery red Japanese maples in lush green parks. The city pulsed with vibrancy. The sidewalks were a mishmash of people from all walks of life and roadside cafes filled to overflowing. She'd been here for a couple of visits since moving to Canada from the United States but had to admit the slower pace on Vancouver Island suited her more.

As the airport came into view, she glanced at her watch. It was going to be close. She wished now she'd thought to ask for Watley's personal phone number, it would have been easier than this cat and mouse game she was playing. She'd left him a message on his office phone and received no reply. And speaking of messages... She checked her cell and smiled at the first one—a heart emoji from Connor.

Miss you already

Aren't you supposed to be working? she replied.

He came back with a quick answer, almost as though he'd been watching his screen. *Doesn't mean I can't miss you*

Who'd have thought the big, tough police detective would be a romantic? And a fantastic kisser. She blushed remembering *all* the places those lips had gone.

You still there? He typed.

She wasn't about to tell him what she was thinking, they'd be lighting up the keyboard if she did. *You snore.* There, that was safe.

You wore me out after all that strenuous activity

Oh, boy. She put a hand to her warm cheek and peeked at the rearview mirror, hoping the cabbie didn't look back. Connor made her feel like a young teenager lusting after the hot cop.

Better save your energy, big guy. I'm planning an encore when I get home

She gripped her phone and held her breath until those three little dots appeared. It had been so long since she'd flirted, the butterflies in her stomach were performing a high-wire act—without a net.

Counting the hours

Her smile was probably dopey, but she didn't care. She paid the cabdriver and hustled through the sliding glass doors for arrivals at the Vancouver International Airport. The airliner coming from Washington D.C. was already disembarking and people milled in the large foyer, some heading toward the luggage carousels while others raced to beat the crowd at the cab stands.

Taking a chance, Julie strode toward the cabs, keeping an eagle eye out for any FBI types. Once an agent, always an agent. Sure enough, a moment later, a dark suit and tie caught her attention. The man had a spare build, dark hair, and walked with confidence. Not wanting to lose him in the growing throng, she raced to cut him off. His eyes widened and he slowed to a stop, shoulders tense.

"Are you Wes Watley?" she hurried to ask, in case he thought she was a threat.

He backed a step away and scrutinized her from head-to-toe. "Depends. Who's asking, and why?"

Julie held out her press credentials. "I'm Julie Crenshaw with the VIBS, Vancouver Island Broadcasting System. A news station," she added for clarity.

"And how does that affect me, Ms. Crenshaw?" He glanced impatiently between her and the quickly disappearing cabs. "I have an appointment. You'll have to excuse me. Call my office and I'll get back to you."

Or not. Julie didn't bother mentioning the messages she'd already left for him to no avail. "Look, I'm here for a friend. My boss. She said you're investigating Michael Saleen and could use…"

"I have nothing to say to the press about an ongoing investigation. As I said, I need to leave and you're in my way, so if you don't mind—"

Sensing she wasn't going to get anywhere, Julie stepped

aside and swung her arm outward. "Be my guest. I'll be seeing you, Mr. Watley."

His gaze sharpened. "Is that a threat?"

Amused at his irritability, but determined not to give up, she shook her head. "Nope. It's a promise."

She stared after him until he jumped into a taxi and took off without a backward glance, then slowly made her way over to a nearby coffee bar. This wasn't going to be as quick and easy as she'd expected. Why did he have to be so obnoxious? Didn't he realize she only wanted to help? A frown marred her forehead. Taylor must have talked to him, hadn't she?

After paying for her coffee, she found a two-seater table and brushed off the seat before sitting. Now that the main deluge of humanity had slipped through its doors, the airport was reasonably quiet, so she pulled out her phone and called Taylor first.

"How did it go?" her friend asked.

Julie snorted. "Depends. Was I supposed to spend more than two minutes in his company?" She took a sip of her steaming coffee and sighed. "Seriously, Taylor, the guy doesn't want me here."

"I was afraid of that. He didn't seem open to suggestions when I called him. But if anyone can convince him, you can."

Sure, she could.

Her lips twisted. If it wasn't for Taylor's friend, she'd leave now, but empathy for the woman held her in her seat. That helpless feeling when she'd lost her own husband was never very far away. If there was anything she could do to help, she had to try.

"I'll give him one more chance. Any idea where I can catch

up to him?" She pulled a pen out of her satchel and turned her napkin over to find a clean square to write on.

"He has an appointment with Sherry this afternoon. I'll call ahead so she knows you're coming." She gave the address and added, "Thanks for doing this, I know it's hard for you."

"Any word on our guy?" Julie tapped the pen on the napkin, leaving a little blue trail along the edge.

"Not yet, still waiting on results from the ME. Ron had an interview with the Carter family—they're distraught."

Julie shivered and the pen ripped a hole in the napkin. If anything ever happened to her children...

"Those poor people. Did Ron get a chance to talk to the boyfriend?" Damn, she wished she was there instead of twiddling her thumbs with this guy.

"Not yet. He's waiting until you get back to town. The tips are already flying in though. We'll have our hands full in the next few days." It took hours of manpower to follow up on every lead, but sometimes the most innocuous piece of information could be *the* clue that solved the case.

"Okay, well I plan on being back tomorrow afternoon as long as Mr. Watley cooperates, so I'll see you then."

"You've got this," Taylor said. "Good luck."

Julie sat back and watched the crowd swirl around her. She needed whatever luck she could get.

CHAPTER ELEVEN

Matt tapped the steering wheel, waiting impatiently while Connor finished texting his girlfriend. This was why he avoided personal relationships, they required too much commitment.

Connor glanced at him and raised a finger. "Almost done," he murmured, attention back on the screen. "Julie won't be back from Vancouver tonight. We had plans," he added as though Matt cared.

He had plans, too. He was going to take the sketch Micah had sent him and spend a few hours combing the camera feeds they'd received, and if that didn't pan out he'd hit the streets himself, because this guy was out there—they just had to find him.

Students hurried back and forth across the university grounds, heavy packs on their backs and arms loaded with binders. Some laughed and talked with their friends, others traveled alone, their expressions lost in thought. City buses wheeled in and out of the pickup zones in an endless stream while gardeners manicured already pristine lawns. With fall in the air, giant orange and yellow maple leaves floated gently to earth, but instead of relaxing him, they only increased Matt's disquiet.

"Sorry about that. Ready?" Connor shoved his cell in his suit pocket and put a hand on the door lever.

"How are we going to handle this?" Matt asked, their failure at the Carter home weighing on his mind.

Connor opened the door. "No pressure. We're just looking for information, not dive into her personal life. Fastest way to lose a witness."

The towering glass and slate gray expanse of the Ocean Sciences building rose before them and again, Matt took note of the many paths snaking through the university grounds. He glanced up and was pleased to see the telltale black boxes signifying video surveillance.

"Catch that?" he asked, nodding toward the light posts.

Connor squinted against the morning sun. "Smart. What do you figure the chances are that they've set those up campus-wide?"

"With our luck? Not good. We'll stop by security after our appointment. Hopefully, they back up their tapes." Matt locked his car and they strode across the parking lot. He wasn't happy with blindsiding Gina Davis at school, but the young woman had proven elusive since her attack and they were running out of options.

Class was just letting out on their arrival. They stood on either side of the open double doors and searched faces until

Matt saw the dark head he was looking for. He stepped forward and intercepted her before she could disappear in the crowd.

"Miss Davis," he called and held up a hand, palm out when she flinched away. "Miss Davis, my partner and I are detectives with the Victoria Police Department. We'd like to have a word with you, please."

Her wounded doe eyes went wide—frightened—and she clutched the binders to her chest. "H... how did you find me?"

Students parted around them, some turning to aim curious glances their way. Matt nodded toward the wall where Connor waited. "Let's get out of the way and I'll explain."

She shook her head and took a step backward, bumping into a tall male. He reached out to save her from falling, but Gina gasped and wrenched her arm free. "Don't touch me," she cried.

He looked from her to Matt, his forehead furrowed. "Hey, I was only trying to help. Take it easy, okay?"

Connor appeared at the boy's side. "She's fine, thanks for your concern. We'll take over now." He flashed his badge and the kid's brows rose into his hairline.

"Yeah, sure. Whatever, man, I don't want any trouble." He turned and beelined down the hall leaving Gina to stare after him like her last hope had just vanished.

"Is there somewhere quiet we could talk?" Connor asked, his voice calm and quiet, eyes kind.

The girl shrugged and hunched her shoulders like a turtle. "I... guess. There's a grass rotunda through those doors." She pointed toward a set of glass-framed doors halfway down the hall. "I have another class soon though, so—"

"We'll make it quick," Matt promised. He led the way, Gina

trailing behind, her shoes shuffling on the floor, and Connor brought up the rear. To anyone watching, they probably looked like worried guardians with a troubled child. Matt felt that way, too. Gina was tiny next to them, maybe five-two to their six feet, and slim. Certainly, no match for someone bent on doing harm. It infuriated him, but he carefully dialed it back, easing a slow breath out as he tugged open the door and waited for the others. Gina had been through a traumatic experience; he didn't want his anxiety ramping up her apprehension of what was to come.

The area wasn't huge, but it allowed students to get outside for a breath of fresh air and some socializing between classes. Granite, wood-topped picnic tables were spread out over the grass and a few leafy trees gave the illusion of privacy while large plate-glass windows looked down on them from towering walls. It reminded Matt of a prison yard.

"How about here?" Connor asked, directing Gina to an unoccupied table away from a group of kids huddled around two boys involved in an intense game of chess.

Gina nodded and scurried over to take a seat with her back to the wall. Matt applauded her safety protocol. Harder for someone to get the jump on you if you see them coming.

Connor undid the single button holding his suit jacket closed and allowed Gina to take note of his badge as he swung a leg over the bench on the opposite side and sat with his back to Matt who stood at the far end of the table so as not to intimidate the girl.

"Miss Davis, Detective Roy and I have been assigned to your case. While we don't wish to cause you any undue distress, it is necessary to ask you a few questions about the night of your attack. Would that be all right with you?" Connor rested his clasped hands on the table and waited, giving Gina the room she needed to process his request.

Matt had seen his partner's interview methods many times in the past and was impressed with his ability to read people. Some, like Gina, required a gentle touch while others were on the receiving end of Connor's bad cop persona—somewhere no one wanted to be.

Gina straightened, then re-straightened the binders she'd set on the table, her fingers trembling. "What is it you want to know?"

"Did you notice anyone odd that day?" Matt interjected. "Someone who made you nervous?"

She glanced up at him as though *he* made her nervous. "N... no, not that I remember."

Frustrated, he leaned on the table. "Try. It's important, Gina."

She glared at him and shoved her neatly stacked books aside. "Do you think I don't know that? I haven't had a proper night's rest since it happened. Every time I fall asleep, I hear his voice, '*I've been watching you, Gina. I know what you did.*'"

Distraught, she rose and took a few steps away from the table, before swinging around to face them. "He knew my name. How did he know my name?" she cried.

"We're not sure, but we plan to find out," Connor said, shooting Matt a glance. "We need a list of all the males in your life, whether they're relatives or the grocery clerk. The more you can give us, the better."

"But why?" Hesitantly, Gina returned to her seat and

pulled out a blank sheet of paper and a pen from her binder. "You can't think someone in my family could have done this?"

Connor sidestepped the question. "You've given us an important lead. These names," he patted the edge of the paper, "could provide us a suspect. We want to get him off the streets so he can't harm anyone else, and you can help us achieve that goal. To take back your life."

Gina slowly nodded and leaned over to neatly write name after name on that snowy white sheet of paper while Matt's heart kicked up a beat. It wasn't random. Their perp stalked his victims. Learned their routines, maybe even integrated himself into their lives.

Another mistake.

We're going to catch you, asshole.

CHAPTER TWELVE

A nxiety poured out of Gina's svelte body. It reminded him of their too-short time together. Heat rose up his chest, filling him with power. His cock stiffened and he moved to the back of the group gathered around a couple of mediocre chess players. His fingers tingled, imagining her life pulsing beneath their tips. He'd made a mistake with her; one he was careful not to repeat. Rushing the experience had cost him the final thrill, and now look, she was yapping to the cops.

His dishwater brown wig itched, but he didn't rub, tempting as it was to draw attention and watch the dumb-ass detectives scratch *their* heads. His brush with cancer had introduced him to the lovely Vanessa who created human hair wigs for patients. Even though they were ridiculously expensive, he'd taken a variety of styles and colors, and then he'd taken her life.

"Hey man, who are you betting on?"

Myself. He looked at the chess players, their concentration locked on the pieces they moved with little finesse. He shrugged. "I'd beat them."

"Pretty sure of yourself, aren't you?" the lanky kid said, giving him a sarcastic look before pushing his way through the crowd to move closer to the players.

"Damn right," he murmured. He frowned. He hated getting mocked for his lisp. In another place, he would've been happy to teach the punk some manners. His gaze slid back to Gina. She was bent over the table, her dark hair a silken slide over her arm as she wrote something on a sheet of paper. The cops looked like a couple of hungry dogs waiting for scraps. It made him curious to know what she was telling them. He wasn't worried, he changed personas for every encounter. They wouldn't catch him.

But he was still interested in what they were saying.

Though his pulse played hopscotch in his veins, he casually strode across the lawn, took a seat at a table under the shade of an elm tree, and opened a book he carried with him as a prop —*David and Goliath* by Malcolm Gladwell. Gina glanced up and looked right through him, just as he expected she would. He wore two layers of clothing for extra bulk and brown contact lenses along with his glasses. He hadn't even recognized himself in the mirror this morning.

The cops were a different story. The one on the bench didn't bother him as much as the tall, dark-haired dude staring at him with crossed arms. That guy looked like he ate razor blades for breakfast. His entire body shouted *don't piss me off*, which of course, immediately made him want to tweak his chain. There was nothing more annoying than a man who couldn't control himself—like his stepfather. It's how he'd learned to think on his feet; no choice when you had a two hundred pound pedophile living in your house.

He shook off the disturbing memories and contemplated his adversaries from beneath lowered lids. What could he do to get those two riled? It came to him in a flash of brilliance. He pulled the burner phone he'd purchased from the pouch of his hoodie. A quick glance across the green showed a good number of students with cells in their hands like extensions of their palms. He scrolled through the photo gallery until he found the one he wanted, took a little creative license and added a call to action the cops couldn't ignore, then click-click, out it went into cyberspace. All he had to do was watch the fireworks begin.

It didn't take long either. He was just returning the phone to his pocket when sweet Gina reached for her backpack. She pulled her phone out of an outside pocket—*dangerous, Gina. Don't you know people can steal your private information that way*—and used the ridiculously easy PIN she'd concocted to access her messages. Her face paled. A second later she turned and puked on the ground close to the glowering detective's shoes. *Ha!* He wished he could have taken a picture of that moment for posterity. Too funny.

The seated cop grabbed her phone and growled something to his partner, holding the photo up for him to see. The big guy stilled, his piercing gaze shooting across the distance separating them from the larger group surrounding the chess players. He started across the grass, shoulders stiff with rage, but his friend grasped his arm, stopping his forward momentum.

"What the hell, man, let me go," the big guy shouted, shaking him off.

This was more entertaining than late-night TV. He grinned and crossed his legs, prepared to enjoy the show.

"Calm down," the other man said. "What are you going to do, grab every phone you can find? You know we can't do that. C'mon, Matt, you're playing into his hands."

That's right, Mattie. Listen to your partner, he's obviously the brains while you're... not. This was going better than he expected. The cops were fighting, and darling Gina was practically hiding under the table.

"Fine," Matt said. "I'll just ask a few questions, get a look at their eyes."

"No. You stay here with Gina. I'll go. I told you you're too emotionally invested in this case. If you can't control your reactions, I'll have you pulled from the investigation—understand?"

Oh, oh. Poor Mattie was in the doghouse. Emotionally invested, huh? He might have to do a little digging on the detective to find out where the bones were buried. After all, if he had a fan, he wanted to know about it. Maybe send the man a gift.

Matt cursed and returned to the foot of the table, his expression granite hard. "Keep holding that over my head and I... Just go," he finished bitterly.

The other man rose, hesitated, said something quietly to the girl, then made his way over to the chess table, passing within a few feet of him with his book. This was too easy. He kept an eye on the detective as he interjected himself into the group, but his attention kept returning to Matt and Gina. Both were worthy opponents in their own way. Gina for having the will to survive the odds, and Mattie for the intensity emanating from him. He wasn't a man to be taken lightly. In a way, they were the same, him and Matt. He was driven to teach his targets a lesson because of their naiveté in a world where evil reigns supreme, and Matt was determined to protect the innocent for the same reason. Commendable, really.

But only one could survive and it wasn't going to be Matt.

A sudden shadow made him look up. The detective stood in front of him, his gaze watchful.

"Detective Connor O'Rourke with VIC-PD. See something interesting over there?" He nodded toward his partner.

Fascinating, is more appropriate. "The young lady looks unwell," he said solicitously, working to control his lisp. "I was contemplating going over to offer a hand, but her friend seems to have it under control." They both looked over to see Matt awkwardly patting Gina's shoulder while grimacing at the undoubtedly nasty smell wafting up from the ground.

"She ate something bad. She'll be fine. Are you studying psychology?"

He lifted his book and grinned. "What gave it away?" See, he could act with the best of them.

"Any chance you were recently on your phone?" the detective asked.

Truth or dare. He loved that game. "No, sir. Finals are coming up and this is a big book to get through. Study, study." The phone in his pocket seemed to grow elephantine in size but he held the detective's gaze and didn't flinch. Yay, him.

"Well, if you hear of anything... odd going on, give us a call, okay?" The detective pulled a business card from his shirt pocket and handed it over. "Anything at all... what was your name?"

"Frank," he said with practiced ease. "Frank Smith. I'll do that, Detective. Happy to help the law anyway I can." Oops, that was a trifle condescending. Good thing the cop was too stupid to pick up on it. He simply nodded and strode back to his friend. They gathered Gina's things together, and with a last, slow gauge of the crowd, ushered her into the school, taking the spark out of his day with them.

He sat and fought against the depression threatening to take hold. It was like this after every connection, though usually it was the eerie silence after his quarry quit breathing that brought it on. Well, the best way to overcome his melancholy was to make plans for another encounter. The thrill of the chase was as good as the buzz from any drug he'd ever tried. And now he had an added incentive—he had an opponent to beat.

CHAPTER THIRTEEN

Matt sat next to a middle-aged university security guard and stared at the video playing out on a desktop computer screen. It was brain-numbing work, but he held onto the hope one of these recordings carried a usable ID of their suspect. Investigators had gone over footage taken from the general area of Gina's attack, but at the time, they hadn't realized they were dealing with a serial offender. With the new information received, he and Connor were going back over the evidence with a fine-tooth comb.

The timestamp on the top right of the screen said it was eight pm, shortly before Gina's final class for the night had ended. She'd told them her routine was to take a path cutting across campus in order to arrive in time to catch the transit bus she needed to get home. There were safer routes, such as the bus lane outside the security building, but at that time of the evening she would need to make several transfers, which made her nervous. It was sadly ironic her careful choices ended up placing her in the crosshairs of a criminal.

After her shock today, Connor had offered to drive Gina home and wait until someone could come over and be with her, so she wasn't alone. Every time Matt thought about the photo and frightening message she'd received; it made his blood boil.

The cops can't save you, sweet Gina. See you soon.

No wonder the girl was scared; the bastard was stalking her.

While Connor had interviewed each of the individuals outside on the grassy rotunda with them, he'd snapped pictures to go over later. Their tech guy, Bob, had come up empty at tracing the number to where the photo originated, but they'd expected that. The perp hadn't made many mistakes to this point, he wasn't going to hand himself over on a silver platter. But he'd given them another clue—Bob had explained even burner phones came with a unique serial number, and given time, he could find out whether their suspect had used the phone to browse the web, make calls, or even if he carried another 'regular' phone with him. Phones constantly communicate with cell phone towers, whether in use or not, and therefore left a digital footprint that could be traced back to the distributor.

"Wait. What's that?" Matt straightened and strained to see the grainy figure moving in and out of the shadows on the video. "Back it up a bit, will you?"

The guard paused the footage and rolled it back a few seconds before hitting play again. This time, they focused their attention on the hunched form in dark clothing, head covered by the hood of his jacket.

"Does it seem as if he's waiting for someone to you?"

The guard shrugged. "Maybe he's got a buddy."

Or maybe he was waiting for Gina.

The seconds rolled at the bottom of the screen until a group of students appeared on the far left. Mystery man faded into the trees to the side of the path as Gina raised her hand in salute and hurried down the trail right past the spot where their suspect had disappeared.

The guard clicked his mouse and another screen opened, just in time to catch Gina striding toward the bus stand, her back bowing under the weight of the backpack riding one shoulder. The bus was scheduled to arrive within the next five minutes, which explained Gina's rash decision to split away from the safety of her classmates.

As expected, the unidentified man stepped out of the brush and followed the young woman, quickly closing the distance between them. He was approximately twenty feet away when Gina stepped under the protective overhang at the bus stop and startled another man, who leaped from the bench he'd been sitting on and his books tumbled to the ground. Gina hurried forward to help as he scrambled to pick them up under the lights of the rapidly approaching bus. The suspect slowed his pace, seemed to hesitate, then faded out of sight.

Gina and the klutzy guy climbed aboard the transit and Matt sat back, frowning. If he hadn't grabbed her here, how did Gina's attacker catch her before she got home? Car? Motorcycle, maybe? Either way, he had to know where she was going, which only led to more questions. Why try on the university grounds where there was more chance of detection? How did he learn her name? A student? Teacher? Ex-boyfriend?

"Can you send us a copy of this footage?" Matt rose. Next stop would be BC Transit. If he was lucky, the customer who rode the bus with Gina had a monthly pass. He was hoping the guy could shed some light on their mystery man.

"I'll have to check with my boss," the guard said with a slight lisp, eyeing Matt's badge clipped to his belt. "I can't see where it would be a problem. Should have it by later this afternoon."

Matt nodded. "Do you know if the same bus operates on a nightly schedule?"

"Yeah, sure. The number four, and the fourteen bus arrives half an hour later."

"That's perfect. Thanks for all your help—appreciated."

The guard rose, too, and held out his hand. "Hope you catch the creep. These are good kids. The young woman didn't deserve what happened to her."

"None of them do," Matt agreed, his thoughts going to his sister and all the other victims who lose their lives to predators.

He left the security office and hesitated a moment. There was a steady flow of students in and out of the UVic Bookstore next door, and he contemplated the value of asking the staff a few questions. He glanced at his watch, surprised to see it was almost two pm. If he wanted to get across town to the BC Transit office, he had to get moving. He made a note in his phone to save the bookstore for another day.

On the way to his Charger, he gave Connor a call.

"What's up?"

Matt's lips quirked. "Can't I just call to say hello?"

"Sure, but then I'd really know something was up," Connor retorted. "You aren't exactly known for small talk."

Well, he couldn't argue with the truth.

"How's Gina?" It still pissed him off that their suspect was toying with her.

"Her friend came over and promised to stay overnight. I posted a couple of patrol members to keep an eye on the house, but it's short term. If we don't get something soon, the captain will cut them loose."

Yeah, it always came down to budget. To hell with human safety. And there he went getting cynical again. Deep down he knew the brass did the best they could with limited resources—it was just as frustrating though.

"I'm heading over to the transit office, want to join?"

"Sounds good. Got a lead?" Connor said.

Matt nodded to a couple of guys checking out his car before opening the door and climbing in. "Fingers crossed, man. Fingers crossed." He tossed his phone on the passenger seat and fired up the engine, but for once the deep-throated growl did nothing to ease the angst building in his chest. They needed to catch a break—and soon.

JULIE CAUGHT up on her emails and wrote down a few notes for her meeting with Sherry Saleen. She looked up when the cab stopped, thanked the driver, and stepped out onto busy Hornby Street. The Saleens lived in one of two penthouses in

The Pacific, a modern thirty-nine story tower with balconies in the clouds on the east and west facades.

Guess she was about to see how the other half lived.

A doorman buzzed Julie in and directed her to a security guard with mountains for biceps sitting behind a chrome and leather counter.

"Do you have an appointment?" he asked in a no-nonsense baritone that rumbled through her chest.

"I do," she said. *As long as Taylor made her call.* "I have a meeting with Mrs. Saleen." He raised an eyebrow as if to say, '*seriously?*' and placed a call to the condo for verification while Julie tried to remain professional and not stick out her tongue like she wanted to.

Rambo dude hung up the phone and gestured toward an elevator sitting on its own off to the left of the large lobby. "Take that one, it goes to the top floor. Door is straight across, past the display table." With those ambiguous directions, he went back to the book he'd been reading—*War and Peace*, no doubt.

Julie entered the mirrored stall and grimaced at her reflection. No wonder the guard had questioned her integrity. She looked as though she'd come through a windstorm—backwards. Between the rush to the airport, her confrontation with Wes Watley, and the return trip downtown, she should have freshened up. *Oh, well.* Too late to worry about it now. She just had time to drag a comb through her hair and apply a coat of lipstick before the doors slid soundlessly open on a grand foyer. Slate tile gave a sleek, stylish look to the room. A huge, round table edged in Tiffany glass held an elegant vase filled with fresh flowers; lavender roses, baby's breath, Asiatic lilies, eucalyptus, white stock, and more. Floor-to-ceiling windows filled the area with light and a stunning vista of Vancouver with the Pacific Ocean shimmering in the distance.

A door opened across the way and a woman, her face pale and drawn, stood in the gap. "Ms. Crenshaw?"

"Julie, please." She hurried around the table, hand outstretched. "I'm sorry we're meeting under these circumstances. Taylor speaks highly of you."

Sherry's expression lightened at the mention of her friend, highlighting beautiful blue eyes. "Taylor and I went to college together." She moved aside and waited for Julie to enter the spacious entry, before closing the door and reengaging the locks. She shrugged under Julie's watchful gaze. "I don't feel safe anymore, even in my own home."

Julie smiled sympathetically and followed her host down a wide hall with floors of Carrara marble and a towering fourteen-foot ceiling to an open concept family room with a large modern kitchen, double island, and attached dining room. The overall impression was one of understated elegance. It was night and day different from Julie's little cottage, but she wouldn't change places for all the tea in China. Her entire house could fit in Sherry's den, but it was a home—the same couldn't be said for this showplace.

Still, it was a beautiful piece of architecture, and she took her time soaking it in until her gaze landed on the man who'd risen from a low-slung leather sofa. Wes Watley.

"What are *you* doing here?" he demanded, brows lowered in annoyance.

"The same thing as you," Julie replied mildly, accepting the dewy glass of lemonade from Sherry with gratitude. "Mmm, this looks delicious, thank you."

Sherry smiled. "From the Meyer lemon tree on the deck. My husband is... was, an avid gardener." Her smile disappeared. "You two know each other?"

"We've met," Julie admitted noncommittally. She wasn't about to get into Watley's rude brush-off earlier.

Apparently, he didn't have the same reservations.

"She accosted me at the airport with an outlandish claim of information that could help your husband," he stated, his expression sardonic.

Why, that... "I never said anything of the sort," she snapped. Turning away from the annoying man, Julie's heart clenched in empathy at Sherry's desperately hopeful gaze. She set her glass on a nearby coaster and took the woman's chilled fingers in hers. "I wish I had the kind of news you want to hear, I truly do. But —" She shot an annoyed glance at Wes. "I do have contacts with the Vancouver Police Department and city hall. They are very good at what they do. I'm sure with Mr. Watley's help you will find your husband." Hopefully, alive.

Sherry squeezed the blood from Julie's fingers, then swayed alarmingly. "I don't..." she mumbled before sinking to the floor.

Startled, Julie dropped to her knees and felt for the woman's pulse. It was there, fluttering like a wild bird against her neck. Her eyes flickered open, then drifted shut, her skin cold and clammy.

"What happened? Should I call 911?" Wes crouched on Sherry's other side and touched her forehead, concern flattening his lips.

"She fainted. Let's give her a minute and then we can decide." Julie had a sneaking suspicion of what was going on, but Sherry might not want anyone else to know before she told her husband. If she got that chance. "Do you think you could carry her to the sofa?"

For once, Wes kept his sarcasm in check. Instead, he carefully tucked his arms under Sherry's too-slim body, lifted her with only a little exertion, and gently settled her on her side on the couch. "I'm going to find a blanket, be right back," he murmured, and strode away.

Julie gingerly sat on the edge of a square mahogany and glass coffee table to watch over her charge. She'd been a fainter with her first pregnancy, as well. It had scared the heck out of Mike, even after the doctor assured him it was normal.

Just as Wes returned with a knitted afghan, Sherry's lids fluttered open and she started to sit up in a daze.

"Whoa, hold on there," Julie said, gently pressing on her shoulder until she relaxed against the cushions. "You passed out on us, so you better stay there for a minute or two."

Wes handed over the blanket and stood with his hands awkwardly shoved into the pockets of his pants. He cleared his throat. "If you're umm, better now, I'll see myself out and we can talk tomorrow, if that works?"

Sherry gave him a tired smile. "Certainly. I'm sorry for the inconvenience. I really do appreciate you coming all this way to help."

Wes looked uncomfortable. "Yeah, well, it's my job, so no bother." He nodded to Julie. "Ms. Crenshaw." He backed away from the sofa, almost tripped over a club chair, and made his escape.

Frustrated, Julie wavered between going after him and staying for Sherry. In the end, she let him go, but they needed to sort things soon—she wanted to get back to her own investigation.

She gave Sherry a reassuring smile. "How are you feeling?"

Sherry shrugged. "You mean other than being eight weeks pregnant with a husband who may, or may not, be dead? I'm great." With that she threw her arm over her eyes and blocked out the world.

Julie could sympathize. There were many times in the past, she'd felt the exact same way. Brushing Sherry's hair off her forehead, she could only hope this story had a happier ending.

CHAPTER FOURTEEN

When Matt turned off Gorge Road East and pulled into an empty stall in the BC Transit parking lot Connor was waiting. He shut down his car, threw his sunglasses on the dash, and joined his partner near the front of the building.

"So, you want to tell me what this is about?" Connor asked, straightening his navy-blue tie.

They were polar opposites in almost every way that counted; he wore jeans and a Henley shirt to work, Connor believed in dressing the part in button down dress shirts, ties, and Oxfords. He lived for the job; Connor worked for a living. Not to say he wasn't dedicated. Connor was a career cop. He'd been in the force for half his life, there wasn't much he didn't know when it came to investigations, whereas Matt made up for his inexperience with determination. Between the two of them, they were a solid team.

"The footage from the security cameras place a guy

following Gina to the transit pickup location on university grounds. The only reason I could figure he didn't grab her right then and there was because another male student was waiting for the same bus. I'm thinking if they regularly use that mode of transportation, they might have monthly passes. If we can acquire the names of students with passes, we might get lucky and find our witness."

Connor squinted into the afternoon glare as a bus pulled into the lot and slowly eased backward into its stall. A moment later, the doors whooshed open and a husky female in city transit attire jumped down and headed toward them, clipboard in hand.

Matt scowled at his friend and was about to turn heel and enter the building without him, when Connor stopped the woman.

"Excuse me, ma'am, we're Detectives Roy and O'Rourke. Could we have a moment of your time?"

The transit driver eyed them suspiciously until Connor showed his badge. Then she relaxed and nodded, her short bob bouncing around her ears. "Sure, but make it quick. I've still got to clock out. Bosses don't like when we file for overtime."

"I understand. We just have a couple of questions for you," Connor said, his expression morphing into that of a benevolent uncle. "I notice you have a route from UVic on your placard. Is that your normal run?"

Matt glanced from Connor to the woman in surprise. How did he miss that?

"Been doing it for fifteen years, or so. Watched a lot of kids go through those doors," she said fondly.

Connor gave her a charming smile. "I imagine. So, you would know the students pretty well then, is that right?"

Matt crossed his arms, slightly in awe of his partner's performance.

The woman rolled her eyes. "Oh, yeah. I could tell some stories you wouldn't believe—not that I would, mind you. I respect a person's privacy, no matter how dumb they're acting."

"Of course," Connor agreed. "Do you by chance know a Gina Davis?"

She closed her eyes, then opened them again and glanced around nervously, as though her bosses were about to pounce out of the bushes any second now. "You didn't hear it from me, okay? Gina is a sweet girl, she didn't deserve what happened to her. I kick myself every day; if I hadn't let her off at that stop, maybe... Anyway, if that's all, I better get going." She clutched her clipboard to her chest.

Connor pulled out one of his business cards. "If you think of anything to help Gina, call us. I know you want to make sure something like this doesn't happen again."

She gingerly accepted the card and shoved it in the front pocket of her pants. "Yeah sure, of course. I hope you catch the creep. Timmy was real torn up after it happened."

Matt straightened. "Timmy who?" he demanded, his pulse racing.

She glared at him. "Timmy Swanson. He rides the same route as Gina. They became friends. He was there that night but got off at the next stop after hers because he was meeting friends at the mall." She raised her chin. "Like I said, those kids like me. They like to talk while I drive—no sin in that."

Connor smiled to calm her down. "No sin at all. Thanks for helping us, Miss?"

"Shearling. And it's Mrs., I've been married for twenty-five years this summer."

"Well, Mrs. Shearling, you've given us lots to go on. We appreciate it, don't we, Detective Roy?" Connor turned steel-gray eyes on him.

Matt coughed back an amused grin. He had a feeling he was about to receive a well-deserved dressing down. "Yes, ma'am. You've saved us a lot of legwork today and congrats on your anniversary, that's a wonderful milestone." *See?* His gaze said. *I can play nice, too.*

Mrs. Shearling gave him a skeptical look, clearly not buying what he was selling. "Yeah, well, hubby says he should be up for parole by now. He's already served a life sentence."

He liked Mr. Shearling already. "Thanks again. Don't forget to give us a call if you think of anything else."

She waved her clipboard in the air and continued into the building and Matt chuckled. "She's a character."

Connor frowned. "One you almost let wriggle off the hook. Did you forget the number one rule in police interrogation? It's easier to get information out of a person of interest if you create a bond with them. That doesn't mean intimidation."

Matt's humor evaporated. "Thanks, Dad. Are you going to ground me now?" He cursed and shook his head. "I screwed up, okay? I realize that, but she caught me off-guard with the kid's name. This is better than I'd hoped for. If we can locate this Timmy character, maybe he can corroborate Micah Miller's description of the suspect." His breathing quickened with anticipation. "We're closing in on him, buddy, I can feel it."

Connor clapped him on the back. "I hope you're right. This case has you tied up in knots. I don't like it."

They separated to head back to their respective vehicles and Matt mulled over his words. It was true, he was deeply involved in the outcome of this investigation, but with his family history he considered that unavoidable. As long as they brought the bastard down, he'd be able to let go of the past and finally move on.

The alternative was untenable.

CHAPTER FIFTEEN

Matt rose at the crack of dawn the next morning and decided to take a jog along the Galloping Goose Trail —partly for enjoyment, partly for research. He wanted a look at the area of the attacks without the distraction of a police presence. He hoped to get a sense of the stalker's habits and what drew him to that location. The more they could read his twisted mind, the better chance they had of taking him down.

He drove to Glen Lake and parked, taking a moment to sit and enjoy the quiet solitude. A light fog hovered over the water while hundreds of songbirds in towering willow and Douglas Fir trees heralded the morning. Dew clung to a lush lawn leading down to a sand beach and playground area. His gaze was drawn to the spot where a young woman had lost her life a scant week ago. Anger tightened his jaw. It was up to him to protect the innocent and he'd failed. It chafed.

He got out of his car and shivered a little. While the autumn days were still sunny and warm, the overnight temperatures held a warning of the changing season. He zipped up his sports jacket, pocketed his keys, and started jogging toward the Galloping Goose access.

At this hour, he had the trail mainly to himself, other than a few early morning runners and bike riders pedaling to work, briefcases attached to their luggage racks. Traffic noise ebbed and flowed as the path led him in and out of the forest, his breathing a foggy vapor and leaves rustling under his worn sneakers. Now and then, a rabbit would bound across the trail in front of him or he'd startle a deer and it would dart through the trees, quickly disappearing from sight. It reminded him of the quarry he chased.

The guy was good at vanishing into thin air.

A wooden foot bridge came into view. Heavy foliage tumbled onto the trail on either end giving the area a picturesque look, but Matt's neck prickled uncomfortably. He slowed to a stop, his senses on full alert.

He eased down to one knee, ostensibly to tie his shoe. Instead, he palmed the sidearm from his ankle holster and slowly rose, his gaze scanning the surrounding forest. The birdsong that had accompanied his run had now fallen silent, further proof something was amiss. Heart rate slowing, the rest of his senses went into hyperdrive. A light breeze tumbled fallen leaves along the paved path and kissed his clammy cheeks. Water burbled nearby, telling him the footbridge wasn't just for show, but that didn't mean it wasn't a trap. His assailant—if there was one—could be waiting for him to take those final steps before attacking when he had nowhere to go.

Only one way to find out.

Gun in hand, Matt approached the bridge as if it were a sleeping dragon ready to explode at any second. Two feet from the point of no return, a twig snapped in the underbrush to his right and he nosedived off the trail, hitting the dust just as a rock winged past and thudded into the trunk of an unsuspecting tree. Breath whistling, Matt lifted his head and tried to locate the suspect. Another missile flew his way, but he managed to get a bead on the culprit as a dark blue jacket ducked into the thick rainforest vegetation and disappeared.

Matt rose and gave chase, his heart jackhammering in his chest. Briefly, he considered the odds of there being more than one but cast it aside to concentrate on narrowing the gap between them. He hoped the rocks meant his prey had no gun as he hurdled a fallen moss-covered tree to find the blue coat only a few feet away.

Without slowing his momentum, he shouted, "Stop, police," and threw himself at the guy's knees. Arms stretched, he wrapped them around jean-clad legs and held on as the perp went down like a felled log. Coming up in a crouch, he double fisted his weapon and aimed at the guy's center mass.

"Stay down. Don't move. Arms behind your back." He shot off the rapid-fire commands and waited until they were obeyed before reaching into his pocket for a zip cuff. He rose and moved quickly to capture the wrists and pat down the body, then stepped back and ordered him to rise.

As the guy rolled over, the hood from his jacket fell off and long blonde hair tumbled out, stunning Matt.

A woman.

The gun wavered and she lashed out, kicking and screaming like a banshee. A foot caught him in the thigh, barely missing his groin, and he cursed as the pain surged up his leg, blurring his vision.

Sensing a victory, she pounced up like a cat and took off through the trees, head down and hands bound behind her back. Matt shook off the agony and raced after her, dumb-founded she'd managed to get the drop on him. He put on a burst of speed and once more crashed into her, this time turning as they went down to protect her from the fall.

"Quit freaking out," he gasped, pinning her to the ground with his legs. "I'm not going to hurt you. Why the hell did you throw rocks at me anyway?" He tried to get a look at her face, but tousled, leaf and stick-filled hair blocked his view. Maybe she was homeless?

"If you hadn't scared me by pulling that gun, I wouldn't have had to," she snarled back like a rabid dog.

That voice... Matt knew that voice. Stunned for the second time in just as many minutes, he grasped her chin and shoved the messy mop from her face. "Taylor?" he said uncertainly. "What the hell...?"

Narrowed ice-blue eyes stared him down defiantly from smudged cheeks. "Detective."

JULIE UNLOCKED the hotel room door and stepped inside with a tired sigh. The curtains were drawn, giving the room, decorated in soft pastel blues, the feel of a sanctuary; just what she needed after a long, discouraging day.

She let the bulky bag slide from her shoulder and land with a soft plop onto the nearest queen bed, then turned on a lamp before sinking onto the other mattress. She should call Taylor and give her an update, but first she had to unwind. The pregnant Mrs. Saleen had affected her more than she'd expected. Three years and her heart still ached with the loss of her baby and its daddy. Sometimes, life wasn't fair. She prayed that wasn't a lesson Sherry would have to learn.

Her phone jangled from the depths of her handbag and she made a dive for it, hoping to hear Connor's reassuring voice. A glance at the screen revealed Wes Watley as the mystery caller. She hesitated before answering, unsure whether she could handle his snarky attitude anymore today.

Just before it went through to voicemail, she picked up. "Hello, Mr. Watley. I'm tired, is there something you need?"

There was some sort of music playing in the background and the chink of glasses. "Wes, please. I won't keep you then," he said. "I just wanted to check up on Mrs. Saleen. How's she doing?"

"She's stressed, of course. Her husband has vanished, and she's scared she'll never see him again. Never get to tell him how much she loves him. How alone she feels without him." Julie blinked back tears and clenched her fist in her lap. "We need to find him before it's too late."

"We? There is no we, kid. Deal is, you connect me to your fed friends, and I do the rest. I work best alone." Wes cleared his throat in her ear. "Look, I know what I'm doing. I'll get Mrs. Saleen her answers—one way or the other."

Kid? Julie would smile if this wasn't so serious and Watley wasn't so aggravating. But in all reality, the Saleen investigation hit too close to home. She'd finally made peace with Mike's death, it was too hard reliving it again through poor Sherry. If she were to lose her child... well, she couldn't, that was all.

"I'll help you on the condition you keep me abreast of the search. Sherry is... frail. She doesn't need any more stress."

"I understand," Wes said. "Look, I can tell you this is part of a larger case I'm working on and there are several leads to follow. I promise to do my best to bring Mr. Saleen back to his wife."

Julie couldn't ask for more than that. Much as she wanted to stay and give support wherever she could, her kids were coming home, she missed Connor, and the Galloping Goose predator was still on the loose. "I'll meet you at VPD headquarters tomorrow morning, eight sharp. Can you make it?"

"See you there. Have a good night, Ms. Crenshaw." Wes said before hanging up and leaving Julie staring at the wall. She loved her job, but sometimes, like tonight, she wished there was no need for broadcast journalists. That the world was peaceful, and danger didn't lurk behind every corner. A fanciful notion from a factual mind. Maybe she was turning a new leaf.

The phone rang again and this time it brought a smile to her lips. "Hello, handsome. I was just thinking about you."

Connor chuckled. "I'd call more often with greetings like that."

Warmth suffused her chest. He had a way of making her

feel like a young girl with her first crush. "It's true. I wish you were here with me. This city is meant to be shared."

"A lover's paradise," he murmured, his voice dropping to a seductive level. "Believe me, I would have liked nothing more. Maybe we could book a weekend for our anniversary."

Julie's breath backed up in her lungs. Was he...?

"You do remember our first date, don't you?" he teased.

Oh. Of course he wasn't proposing over the phone. Or at all, really. It was too soon anyway. They'd only been together a matter of months. Then why was she so disappointed?

Forcing a light laugh, she rose, paced to the window, and pulled the curtain aside. The Vancouver skyline lit up the early evening horizon, compounding her loneliness. "How could I forget? You interrogated me at the police station and we had a moment." More than a moment. He'd been kind and considerate and she'd... kissed him. His palm sure, but still. Not exactly the reaction of a grieving widow.

"That was when I knew you were going to change my life."

"You mean complicate it," she said, thinking of the fright they'd been through when her son ran away from home.

"Hey, I'm a detective, remember? We thrive on complications. Speaking of which, how did your appointment go?"

"Other than butting heads with an arrogant investigator? It was fine. Taylor's friend is worried sick about her husband, but there's still hope, so she's hanging on. I wish there was more I could do."

"I could look into it from my end, if you want?"

He was offering to step out on a limb for her; no wonder she'd fallen so hard for him. "No, but I appreciate the offer. I'm connecting him to some good cops in the morning, they'll find Mr. Saleen." *Please let him be alive.*

He hesitated. "I miss you."

She let the curtain fall and leaned against the wall. "Me, too. See you tomorrow?"

"Count on it," he said. "Sweet dreams."

"Sweet dreams," she answered and ended the call. Suddenly, an early night seemed like a good idea.

CHAPTER SIXTEEN

Matt stared at the woodland waif who'd almost unmanned him and tried to wrap his head around the fact that it was Taylor Monroe. The last time he'd seen her, she'd been wearing a form-fitting black dress and swanky heels —oh yeah, and she hadn't been trying to kill him.

Out of breath, and still annoyed she'd gotten the drop on him, he leaned against the trunk of a cedar and eyed his adversary. She stared back, defiance in the sensual lines of her body.

"So... are you going to tell me why you were hiding in the bushes like a stalker?" he asked, drawing out his knife but making no move to untie her hands. She could stew for a while.

Her eyes flashed blue fire. "I am *not* a stalker and you darn well know it, Detective Roy." She blew at a straggly chunk of hair hanging in her face. "Are you going to let me go, or clean your nails with that thing?"

Matt chuckled. "Feisty, aren't you? You'll be lucky if I don't lock you up for assaulting a police officer. You could have knocked me out with one of those rocks."

"I wasn't that lucky," she mumbled, turning awkwardly so he could cut the tie around her wrists. The moment it snapped loose, she skittered a few feet away and rubbed the red skin. "How am I supposed to explain this at work?"

Matt shrugged, though he did feel guilty for hurting her. "Crazy sex games?"

"Ha, as if." She snorted. "I'd need to have sex first."

Matt jerked, certain he'd misheard, or she was exerting that sarcastic tongue of hers, but no, she wasn't even looking at him. Her attention was focused on removing the bits and pieces of forest debris embedded in her long gold hair like a crown of thorns—fitting, if the comment about her sex life was true. And now he couldn't get images of her in the throes of passion out of his head.

He shifted uncomfortably and tried to redirect his thoughts. "You haven't answered me yet. Why were you off the beaten path? And don't tell me it was a nature hike, either."

She glanced at him through narrowed eyes and went back to dusting herself off. "Who made you the trail police? Oh wait, maybe you are now. I heard you like to ruffle feathers. Could be your boss had enough and put you where you couldn't get into trouble—or so he thought."

"You must be a real riot at parties," Matt said, amused. "Are you always this defensive?" He pulled up his knees and got ready to enjoy the show.

He didn't have long to wait.

Taylor slowly bent at the waist, giving him an eyeful of soft, white skin peeking out the top of her shirt before a cascade of musty, damp leaves splatted his chest.

"Hey," he sputtered, jumping to his feet to swipe at the mess. "This is my good suit."

She smirked. "You're a real comedian. How does it feel to kiss the dirt?"

He wanted to kiss something, but it wasn't dirt. She was the most aggravating woman he'd ever met. "You do remember I'm a cop, right?"

"Ewww," she said, waving jazzy hands on either side of her head. "Is the big, bad policeman going to arrest me?"

Tempting, oh so tempting.

"Can we get back to what you are doing here? Because if it's to investigate the Galloping Goose Killer, I just might arrest you for your own good." She was a news producer, she should know better than to take such a foolish risk. A couple of bikers rode by on the path above them with no sign of noticing anyone in the ditch line. It only emphasized how dangerous it was for a woman to be out here on her own.

"I see you've adopted our label for this guy," she said, admitting to nothing. "So we *are* dealing with a serial killer then?"

He could practically hear the *Breaking News* report already. "I never said any such thing. While it's true two women have recently died on or near the Galloping Goose network, it has yet to be proven the crimes were committed by the same perpetrator, never mind a repeat offender. As I told your ace reporter last week, this is an ongoing investigation. Where is she, anyway? I'd expect her out here snooping long before you."

She raised a sandy brow. "Are you trying to tell me I don't

have what it takes, Detective? Because I could teach you a thing or two."

His turn to raise a bemused brow. "Be careful, I might just take you up on that one day." He wouldn't mind receiving lessons from Taylor Monroe. On anything.

She frowned, but a delicate blush painted her cheeks a pearly pink. "You're insufferable. Julie's in Vancouver for a couple of days on a different matter. I was hoping I could find a missed piece of evidence—which I would have turned over to your team—to help with her story. She's doing me a big favor."

Connor hadn't mentioned his girlfriend was on the lam. No wonder she wasn't driving them crazy over the latest victim. Her reporter's nose was legendary, normally she would have been pestering them nonstop.

"And did you?" he asked, crossing his arms and waiting for her to lie.

Her forehead furrowed and she gazed around them impatiently. "Did I what, find anything? Don't you think I would have told you if I had?"

Not on your life. "Withholding evidence is a felony, Taylor. You may want to rethink your answer." She'd given herself away by not looking at him while fibbing, now the question was whether or not she'd come clean.

At first, it seemed as though she was going to bluff her way out, but then she huffed out a frustrated breath and shook her head. "You're aggravating, do you know that?"

He watched as she strode toward the rocky outcropping where he'd first seen her and reached down between the stones to pull out a battered looking book. Disappointment rolled through him. He wasn't sure what he'd anticipated, a piece of clothing, maybe? But a discarded hardcover with weather-beaten pages wasn't it.

She carried it back, holding it gingerly between her finger-tips, her face expectant. When he didn't immediately reach for it, she frowned. "Well?" she said. "Aren't you even going to look at it?"

"This could have been dropped by anyone," he answered, even as he pulled out a pair of latex gloves and dutifully tugged them on.

"Yes, but it isn't from just anyone," she crowed, handing him the tattered book. "Look at the inscription."

Puzzled, he opened the cover.

> I've watched you from afar, yet you've never
>   noticed me.
> But that's okay, you will.
> Our time is near.
> Are you ready, my dear?

Matt slowly raised his eyes and met Taylor's eager gaze. Her job was to find the story and report on it, and she may have just found the evidence they needed to crack this investigation wide open. How was he going to keep her from revealing what she'd discovered?

CHAPTER SEVENTEEN

Julie set up the appointments with VPD and city hall authorities, attended the meetings with the sarcastic Wes Watley, then hurried to make her flight to Victoria. She'd assured Wes and Mrs. Saleen she would keep in touch, but truthfully, she could work better from home than in the big metropolis. Besides, it was obvious Wes didn't appreciate her input and she had her own investigation to catch up on.

When Taylor called, she mentioned something about a book she'd found alongside the Galloping Goose that could be a possible lead in the case, while Ron had a meeting with the Friedman family lined up. It sounded as though things were speeding along on the GGK situation and she wanted to be back in the thick of it.

Thirty minutes later, the floatplane touched down in Victoria harbor and Julie released a relieved sigh. She eagerly searched the wharf for Connor and smiled when his tall form came into view. It was the middle of his workday, so he'd warned he might not make it, but she'd hoped he could find the time. And here he was, looking all hot cop in his dark pants and light blue button down open at the neck. His auburn hair glinted with copper tints in the afternoon light and more than one person on shore took note of his commanding figure.

The pilot taxied up to the dock and shut down the engine before glancing back. "Beautiful day for a flight. I hope you enjoyed your ride to the island." His practiced smile was obvious, but friendly.

Julie's two cabin mates, a newly married couple, gushed over the view they'd had of the Gulf Islands in the Strait of Georgia. "We're so happy we decided to come here for our honeymoon," the young woman said, her arm hooked around her beaming husband's. "We can't wait to go whale watching."

Julie grinned at their exuberance. She remembered when she and the boys first arrived in Victoria and were taken with the quaint charm of the small city and its citizens. It made starting over after Mike's death easier for all of them.

The pilot shimmied between the seats and opened the door, allowing fresh sea air to infiltrate the cabin, while he chatted with his guests. A few minutes later, they were anchored in place and able to disembark.

Julie accepted the pilot's offered hand to descend the stairs, and with a quick thanks, strode into Connor's waiting arms. "I'm glad you could make it," she said, lifting her head for a quick kiss. "Did you miss me?"

"Do you have to ask?" he murmured, his nose buried in her

hair. "Only every second." His kiss was longer, more languid. "I wish I could take the rest of the afternoon off."

The butterflies taking flight in her stomach agreed with him. "Could I persuade you?" She fondled the curls on his nape and was gratified to feel him shudder.

"You're tempting me to play hooky, but I can't. Your boss found an important piece of evidence. It's all boots to the ground now." He squeezed her close, then took her hand to stroll toward his car. "Rain check?"

Any time, any place. Aloud she teased, "We'll see."

Smiling, she accepted his opening the door for her and waited until he climbed behind the driver's seat to ask about the GGK. "Did I miss much while I was gone? Tell me you caught the Galloping Goose Killer and put him behind bars where he belongs."

Connor started the car and lowered his window to the shrill cry of seagulls wheeling overhead. "You have no idea how much I wish that were true." He brushed her cheek with his thumb, sending her pulse fluttering. "You know I can't discuss police business with a reporter—even you."

The dancing in her veins slowed. She knew he didn't mean to sound patronizing, but... it was annoying, nonetheless. She moved away from his hand to remove her jacket and get her temper under control.

He sat back and eyed her. "Are you angry?"

"No," she muttered. "I enjoy getting put in my place by my boyfriend. It's... enlightening."

Connor sighed and turned the idling engine off. "That wasn't my intention. Can we start again? Please?"

She folded her coat over her arm and met the regret in his eyes. "I'm sorry. It's just that I get tired of fighting career discrimination around every corner, I didn't expect it from you."

"Jules." He grasped her hand. "I have nothing but the deepest respect for what you do. It must be incredibly hard to research the stories you go after and then strike the right note with your viewers to inform them without causing pandemonium." He kissed her palm before letting go. "I don't want our jobs to come between us, do you?"

The thought of losing Connor tightened her throat. The boys adored him, and she... she couldn't bear to let him go. "That's the last thing I want. I shouldn't have asked such a leading question without it being official. It's just, Taylor mentioned finding a book along the trail and she seemed so excited I thought maybe..."

The honeymoon couple strolled by hand-in-hand, their love visible for all to see. Would she ever find that soul-deep connection again? She thought she had with Connor, but now she wasn't so sure. Maybe he was after casual, while she... she'd fallen hard for the detective. *Oh, boy.*

"You're right, I overreacted. Besides—" He grinned and she startled, thinking he'd read her thoughts. Instead, he said, "Matt is still stewing over that one. I'll let Taylor tell you the story, suffice to say he learned a valuable lesson from your boss."

He turned in his seat to face her, enthusiasm turning his gray eyes magnetic. "The book has an inscription, one we're almost sure was written by our perp."

He leaned forward and lowered his voice. "This has to stay off the record, okay?" He waited for her to nod. "Handwriting is defined by twenty-one unique characteristics. There are dimensions, proportions, spacing—a forensic examiner can use these factors to connect writing to a person. Do you understand what this means? We're another step closer to catching this guy, Jules. It's all coming together." He slapped his palms on his knees for emphasis.

Julie was less enthused. "Unless he sends you a written confession, I don't see how this helps. Is it even allowable in court?"

"That's up to the judge, but it's getting accepted as forensic evidence in a lot of cases. As to the writing, if we can narrow our search, which we're close to doing, we can gather proof to put before the courts." He sat back and stared at her. "I thought you'd be happier about this?"

She brushed away her misgivings to smile at him. "I am. I realize it's another piece of the puzzle. I guess I just want a clear sign pointing to the killer. Silly, right?"

He reached across the console and hugged her close. "After what you've been through, not silly at all. Don't worry, we'll catch him." He nuzzled her ear.

She shivered, as much from his words as his touch. She hoped it went as smoothly as he predicted, but in her experience, murderers rarely did what was expected.

CHAPTER EIGHTEEN

Matt tuned out the busy police station and placed a call to Micah Miller. He'd sent her an email a few days earlier updating the information they'd received from interviewing Gina Davis, and now he was hoping she could include her take on the handwriting they'd found and wether it could belong to their guy. His gut said yes.

"Hello?" Micah said, her voice distracted.

"Ms. Miller, it's Matt Roy. Detective Roy from the VicPD in Canada. I don't mean to rush you, but—"

"But you are, anyway," she said sarcastically. "That's okay, Detective, I'm used to dealing with impatient types. I imagine you're looking for my findings on the data you sent me."

His lips quirked at her no-nonsense tone. "Yes, ma'am. I realize I haven't given you much time, but anything you could add to our investigation would be appreciated."

Matt got an eyeful of his partner's grim expression when Connor wandered in and took a seat at his desk.

"*What's wrong?*" he mouthed.

Connor shrugged, leaned back, and kicked a polished shoe onto the edge of his desk.

Matt frowned at the uncharacteristic movement, but Micah's next words pulled his attention.

"Right, let's get to the handwriting sample first. As you know, this is not my wheelhouse, so I took the initiative to call a friend of mine for his opinion. Professor Mills is a master graphologist and had interesting insights to share.

"The large letters suggest the writer wants attention. You may have noticed there is no slant to the words; this says he/she is ruled by logic and is unemotional. The light pressure backs this up, the person moves easily from place to place and doesn't wear themselves out emotionally.

"This is where it got interesting for me; the looped T in the upper zone, as Professor Mills calls it, tells us your suspect could be susceptible to criticism and is likely paranoid. The fact that the letters are not connected means he/she is methodical and makes decisions carefully. And lastly, the even spacing tells us he knows his boundaries and strictly adheres to them."

Matt jotted down everything she said and nodded. The analysis fit with the picture he'd drawn in his head of the guy they were looking for. "This is helpful. Thank you, Micah."

Connor dropped his foot and leaned forward, hand out to receive the notes he'd taken. Matt passed them over and was relieved to see interest overtake whatever was bothering his friend.

"Now, as to the other matter," Micah said in his ear. "This escalation in behavior worries me."

She wasn't the only one concerned. "Hang on," Matt said. "I'll set you on speaker so my partner can hear."

"As you know, I can only predict the age of your suspect, as well as other factors such as lifestyle and health using the Snapshot DNA Phenotyping System. Advances in genomic technology have made it affordable to read sequences of DNA from a very small sample. This data contains much of the genetic blueprint that differentiates between people's appearance. Couple that with the handwriting analysis and cat and mouse game he seems to be playing with you and it adds up to the profile of a highly intelligent, meticulous man, mid-forties, with little or no family ties.

"The first line in the quote actually tells us a lot about this man's mental state. *I've watched you from afar, yet you've never noticed me.*

"He feels a connection to his victims and is frustrated that it is one-sided. He is self-confident and this triggers the predator inside of him. He'll make her notice him.

"A man like this has no compunction and kills with ease.

"He's done this for a while and knows how to camouflage himself. I've taken the liberty to draw up a series of sketches defining different characteristics he may use to change his appearance. I've emailed you the files and will send composite drawings by overnight express." She hesitated, then said, "Be careful, gentlemen. He won't come in easily."

Micah hung up and Matt cursed. "I was afraid of this. He's been out there, committing who knows what, for a decade or more without getting caught. He's smart. Maybe smarter than us."

Connor shook his head. "Where's that negative attitude coming from? You're usually the one-man pep squad in our unit. Don't give up, we'll get him."

"Yeah," Matt challenged. "Okay, oh wise one. How are we supposed to accomplish the impossible, huh?" He'd been chasing his sister's killer for ten years and was no closer than the day she died. He hated not being able to give her the closure she deserved.

"Well, sitting around here moping won't get us very far," Connor said, rising from his chair. "I'm going to pay the medical examiner a visit and see what he's come up with for our last victim. Have you caught up with Alexander Friedman yet?"

Emily Carter's boyfriend, the one she'd argued with shortly before her death. "Not yet. I'll head over to his place first and meet you at the ME's office later."

Connor tapped his arm as they strode out of the station together. "You just want to get out of visiting the clinic."

No denying that. It was more than the exam that bothered him though. The oppressive, sterile feel of the place got to him. There was no coming back once you ended up on the doc's slab. Matt wasn't in a hurry for it to be him going under the knife.

"Hey," he called as Connor began to walk away. "You want to tell me what had you so upset earlier?"

Connor hesitated, then shrugged. "Julie and I had a disagreement. We'll work it out."

In other words, none of his business. Matt was fine with that. He made a crappy advice councillor anyway. He raised his hand to wave his partner off and turned toward the Charger. Easier to love a car, it wouldn't turn on you.

———————

JULIE SHOOK off the sour note between her and Connor, had a quick shower, watered her dying African violet, and drove to the VIBS station. She was anxious to find out just what it was Taylor had found.

The cavernous building echoed with the hustle of a busy television studio. People moved from section to section trading ideas while fans worked to keep the equipment cool, and papers rustled. Behind the scenes, it was a beehive of activity. Enter the realm of the recording studio however, and other than the camera crew and anchors reading from teleprompters as scenes played out on giant screens behind them, all was church quiet. Julie liked her job as anchor of the evening news, but she lived for the thrill of going after a story. It was the next best thing to becoming a private investigator, and in some ways even better. Doors opened for her that Mr. Wes Watley would never get through.

Ron stopped her on her way to Taylor's office, his green eyes alight with curiosity. "So, how was the big city, Crenshaw? Checking out new job prospects?"

She avoided his Harlem Globetrotter sized feet to place her bag on the desk, dodging his question to ask, "Did you get out to the Carter house? What did they have to say?"

"Hello to you, too," he said, crossing one long leg over the opposite knee. "Yes, to the Carters. Now you tell me something, that's how this works." He grinned.

She should have asked for a new partner while she was gone, that's what she should have done. Ron knew how to push all of her buttons. It's a good thing he was a decent reporter, and a nice guy—when he wasn't driving her crazy.

Sighing, she leaned her butt against the desk. "I was on an errand for a friend, okay? Now tell me what you've got."

He gave her a skeptical look, then reached to grasp the file next to her purse. "Typed, sealed, delivered. I know how anal you are about reports."

Julie ignored the wise crack to take the folder and leaf through the pages inside. Most of it consisted of the expected responses from distraught parents mourning the loss of their daughter, but one section of the interview caught her attention.

She glanced at Ron, then back to the questions. "You talked to the Carters' son? He doesn't seem to think this was a random attack."

Ron leaned forward and rapped the papers she held. "He says she was getting weird messages on her phone for a couple of months leading up to the confrontation. She asked him to look into it because he's taking a computer design course at school, but he put it off as a gag—said he was bogged down with class assignments. It cut him up pretty bad."

Julie nodded, empathy for the teen a heavy weight in her chest. "Any chance he can remember what the notes said?"

"His father showed up just as he was about to say something and shut the interview down." Ron frowned. "That guy gives off a weird vibe. You'd think a father who'd just lost his daughter would be happy to do whatever he could to get her killer behind bars, instead he acts as though we're accusing *him* of the crime."

Maybe they should be. Julie tapped her chin with the file. "Do we know anything about Mr. Carter? I mean, he's a bigwig in town, obviously, but do we have any personal information on him and his family?"

Ron grabbed a pen from his desk, next to Julie's, and scribbled some notes on a legal pad. "I think we did a story on him a couple of years ago, but I'll have to check archives."

"Okay, good." Julie straightened and dropped the folder on her desk. "I need to see Taylor for a few minutes and then we can head out to our appointment with Alexander Friedman." She glanced at the thin watchband circling her wrist. "Three o'clock, right?"

Ron rose, curiosity lighting a torch in his eyes. "Yep, three pm at Beacon Hill Park. He didn't want to meet at his house." He nodded toward the producer's closed door. "Sure you don't want me to go with you for moral support?"

And to find out what we've been up to, Julie thought. Reporters had a knack for sniffing out a story. But not this time. If Taylor wanted the crew to know about her friend, she'd make an announcement at her own discretion.

"Nah, I'm good, thanks. Just be ready to leave when I come out." She started across the floor, then glanced back. "Don't worry, Ron. I'm not trying to steal your seniority."

With that, she carried on toward Taylor's office. It was hard being the newbie on the team, even though she'd been here a couple of years now. The competition was fierce. They all worked well together, but there was always an itch between the shoulder blades, as though a knife might plunge through at any moment. And in her case, it had.

She shivered under an onslaught of goosebumps and gave a quick rap on the door before letting herself in.

Taylor looked up from the organized chaos she called a desk and gave a tired smile. "You're back."

Julie was alarmed by how pale she looked. The hours could be brutal at the station, but she had a feeling something else was bothering her friend.

She closed the door behind her, blocking out the noise, and took a seat in one of the straight-backed guest chairs, obviously meant to deter people from overstaying their welcome.

"You look like hell," she stated bluntly. "What's wrong?"

Taylor's smile froze and she stiffened slouching shoulders. "I have no idea what you're talking about."

Julie gazed at her skeptically. "Really? We're going to play that game? Okay, tell me about your brush with Detective Roy then."

Taylor frowned. "How did you...? Never mind, I suppose he had a grand time rehashing the whole sorry affair."

Oh, oh. Someone's pride had been injured. "Actually, Connor mentioned you and Matt had a run in, but if I wanted any more info I had to talk to you." Julie raised her hands and grinned coaxingly. "So, here I am. Spill."

"Well, at least I'm not a complete laughingstock yet. I'm sure it's only a matter of time." Taylor dragged her hands through her hair and Julie was amazed clumps didn't come out. "Have you ever done something you regretted? Like, deeply regretted?"

"Come on, it can't be that bad." This was getting more and more interesting.

"Oh, it's worse," Taylor mumbled. "I assaulted a police officer and almost robbed him of his family jewels."

Wait, what? Julie stared at her in wide-eyed surprise. Mild mannered Taylor resorting to violence? Now this she had to hear. "How in the world did you come to attack Matt? He's twice your size!"

Taylor looked up and glared. "You don't have to tell me that. He darn near knocked the wind out of me when he tackled me to the ground."

Julie stuttered out a nervous laugh. "I think you better back up and start at the beginning. This sounds kind of kinky at the moment."

Taylor stared at her, affronted. "Trust me, I wouldn't let that man near me voluntarily with a ten foot pole." She sighed and rose to pace the short space from her desk to the wall and back again. "I thought it would be a good idea to go out to the woods near Glen Lake and see if I could find any leads for when you came back from Vancouver. I live out that way, so I just jogged the Galloping Goose, keeping my eyes open for anything of interest.

"Sure enough, near the footbridge I saw a flash of red and stopped for a better look." She rubbed her arms, her brows furrowed. "One minute I was leaning over the bridge for a better look and the next someone shoved me from behind and sent me tumbling into the gully."

Julie gasped. "Oh, my gosh. Are you hurt? Did you call the police? Did you get a look at who did it?" The questions poured out with her fright. Taylor could have died while trying to help her get a story.

She rose and hurried around the desk to wrap her arms around her friend. "What were you doing out there alone?" She'd stressed during her news broadcast how important it was for anyone, man or woman, to travel with a companion and here Taylor was, ignoring that basic safety measure.

Taylor leaned into the hug, then sniffled and let her go. "I know, I'm an idiot. That point was made clear to me several times that day. Not only did I find myself sprawled on the bank of the creek, but then I heard someone coming and thought it was whoever attacked me. I grabbed a couple of good-sized rocks and scrambled to hide, but the guy saw me and gave chase. I flung the rocks and ran for my life. I thought I was going to escape right up until he knocked me off my feet and after a scuffle, tied my hands behind my back."

She scrubbed at her still-red wrists. "That's when I discovered my abductor was actually my dubious rescuer—Detective Roy."

Julie shook her head, stunned by this turn of events. Connor hinted it was quite the story, he wasn't kidding. "Wow. Considering the circumstances, it seems weird to say you're lucky Matt came along, but jeez, Taylor, it could have been so much worse. Did you tell him someone pushed you?"

"No," she said. "I looked like a big enough idiot. I wasn't about to make it worse." She raised her chin. "It was probably a prankster, just let it go. I've learned my lesson." She resumed her seat at the desk. "Now, do you want to hear about the book I found?"

CHAPTER NINETEEN

Matt pulled up in front of an older two-story bungalow on Bay Street and shut his car off. As he strode toward the robin's egg blue front door, he took note of the overgrown garden and the home's peeling paint. These old houses took a fair amount to maintain and if you didn't keep them up, they ended up looking tired and forgotten. Quite the contrast compared to the Carter estate. It made him wonder if there was friction between the families.

He climbed the stairs to the wide front porch, knocked on the door, and jumped back when a dog barked rabidly from the other side. The childhood scar on his leg throbbed in sympathy. Matt could handle small mutts—just. But when it came to anything over fifty pounds, he quaked.

The doorknob turned and his heart exploded, his hand automatically going to the weapon resting in his shoulder harness as he braced for impact. A black snout and large canines pushed through the gap created by a heavy-duty chain holding the door in place. An elderly woman peeked over the German Shepherd's head.

"Can I help you?" she asked, her hand between the animal's ears seemingly enough to settle him down.

Matt wasn't taking any chances. He kept his hand on his gun and away from those teeth. "Excuse me, ma'am, I'm Detective Roy with VicPD. I'd like a word with an Alexander Friedman, please?"

"Oh," she said, releasing the chain to open the door wider. "Sit, Sam," she told the dog and he listened, plunking down on the hardwood floor. His attention remained fixed on Matt, though, and Matt divided his gaze between the kindly looking woman and her guardian.

"You're the third one to ask after him today," she stated, using her cane to step onto the porch. "Is my nephew in some kind of trouble?"

Third one? That didn't sound good. "We just have a few questions for your nephew, Mrs....?"

"Harper. Alex's mom was my sister, bless her soul." She absently patted Sam's head. "We lost her to cancer three years ago. It's been hard on poor Alexander."

"I understand. It's not easy to lose a parent." Matt vowed to call his own mom and dad when he got home—it had been a couple of months. "I won't keep him long, is he here?"

Mrs. Harper looked at him, confused. "Who, dear?"

Matt suppressed a groan. "Alexander, your nephew."

"Oh, of course. No, he left a while ago. Said he was meeting someone in Beacon Hill Park. Do you know where that is?" Mrs. Harper pointed out a vague direction down the street.

Matt smiled. "I think I can find it. Thanks for your time. It was nice to meet you, Mrs. Harper."

"You too, dear. It's not often a handsome young man comes calling." She winked and tapped her cane. "Come on, Sam. Time for *Judge Judy*. That's such a good show," she confided in Matt. "You could learn a thing or two from her."

"Yes, ma'am, I'm sure I could." Matt hurried down the steps before she invited him in. "Have a nice day."

"I'm too old for anything else," she said, tapping the cane to get Sam moving.

Matt grinned. She was a character, that one. He was almost to the gate when he remembered what she'd said. He turned and caught her before she disappeared inside.

"Mrs. Harper," he called. "You mentioned I wasn't the first to ask after your nephew. Can you tell me who else was here?"

She hesitated, then gave a faint nod. "Only one stopped by, a man who was quite rude. I didn't tell him where my Alexander had gone, and Sam persuaded him to leave."

Good for Sam. He might learn to like dogs again after all— might. "And the other person?" he prompted.

"Oh, that was a pleasant young woman on the phone. I thought I told you; that's who Alex went to meet." She tipped her head. "If that's all, I'm missing my show..."

"Yes, of course. Thanks, again," he called to her departing back. Sam followed close behind his mistress, his interest in Matt gone.

So, Alexander was a popular guy—interesting. He had a

good idea who the 'nice young woman' could be, and if Julie Crenshaw had chased down his person of interest, he'd have a few choice words for her. It was the other guy that had him concerned. Who was he and what did he want with Alexander?

———————

JULIE SAT on the other end of the wooden bench from the nervous teen who'd agreed to meet with her—on his terms. Alexander Friedman was a gangly youth, with a whiskery jaw and a cantankerous expression.

"I don't know what you want from me, I don't know anything." He shoved his hands in his hoodie and glared out to the sparkling blue Pacific.

Her arms ached to give him comfort, though he wouldn't appreciate it. His attitude reminded her of her son's after the passing of his father. It had taken Dustin a long time to make peace with his loss—she had a feeling Alexander felt things just as deeply.

Wishing Ron hadn't been called to another appointment, she reached into her cavernous purse and pulled out a takeaway bag. "I'm starving, you?" She removed a couple of chicken wraps and a bottled water for each of them and set his on the seat between them. He gazed at the offering, then up at her. Julie shrugged and took a bite of her wrap. "I took a chance on what you might like."

Just then his stomach decided to rumble.

"Go on," she said. "I can't eat two."

Tall, golden grasses swayed in the breeze while waves

gently kissed the rocks on the shore below them. It was a sunny, serene type of day and Julie wished she wasn't here to talk about another death. She was still recovering from Taylor's call; Michael Saleen had been found. He'd apparently driven over a cliff on his way home and died.

"I'm sorry you lost Emily, I know it must be hard." She glanced sideways in time to see him freeze, the chicken wrap halfway to his mouth. He swallowed hard, then shrugged and continued with his bite.

"We weren't that close," he mumbled around the food.

Julie opened his water for him and handed it over. "Still, it must have been a shock." Her research had shown the two were in fact a couple and had been for months, but if that's the stance he wanted to take, it was between him and God.

"She was dumb to run off like that. I told her I would give her a ride if she'd just settle down for a minute." He crumpled up his wrapper and took a drink of the water before getting up to throw his garbage into a nearby trashcan. When he turned back, grief made his eyes flat. "She was pregnant, you know. That's why we had the fight. I told her she was lying, and now she's gone."

Julie sucked in a distressed breath. "Oh, honey. You couldn't have known. Please don't blame yourself for what happened."

He swore and flung the bottle across the field. "Who else should I blame?" he yelled, his expression tormented. "I let her go. It's my fault she's dead." He crumpled to his knees and hung his head.

Heartsick, Julie set her wrap aside and hurried to his side.

She leaned over and placed a comforting arm around his shoulders. "When my husband died, I felt the same way. If only I hadn't taken his attention from the road, he would have seen the car coming straight at us and avoided the accident. It took me a long while to accept the loss, but I realized he wouldn't want me to go through the rest of my life condemning myself for what happened. Emily wouldn't want that for you either, Alexander."

He nodded, wiped wet cheeks on his sleeve, and shifted away from her hold. "Is that why you became a reporter?" he asked. "To help people like you?"

Julie tucked her hair behind her ear, surprised at his insightful comment. "You know what? I never thought of it like that, but maybe you're right. It makes me feel like I'm doing something worthwhile. Something that will make a difference in people's lives." She moved back to the bench for her water bottle. "That's why I wanted to see you today." She took a drink and looked him in the eye. "The person who killed Emily has hurt other women as well, Alexander. I need your help to make it stop."

He rose and strode to where he'd thrown his bottle, returning to place it in the garbage can. Julie waited, giving him time to think over what she'd asked of him. This part of the park was quiet. Only one other person had passed by on the trail since they'd been there. She shivered and glanced around, suddenly uneasy.

"It's Alex," he said. And at her quizzical look, "Alexander is my dad. Most people call me Alex. What kind of help?"

Relieved he hadn't turned her down flat, Julie pulled a notepad and pen from her satchel. "Do you remember if Emily was upset or worried about anything in the days leading up to—"

"She said some guy was sending her weird messages. He left notes in her school locker, too. At first she thought it was me, you know, being a secret admirer or something." He blushed. "But then she got creeped out. I told her to take it to the security office and get them to look into it."

"Did they?" Julie questioned, writing down the information. Connor had mentioned something about the security office, as well. She made a note to go there herself tomorrow. When he didn't answer, she looked up. "Alex?"

He flopped onto the bench, long legs stretched in front of him and eyes trained on the horizon. "I didn't ask her, okay? Sh... stuff was happening at home and I forgot about it until now. What kind of boyfriend does that?"

"The kind who is young and has a lot on his shoulders. Don't beat yourself up. This is great, just the kind of information I need. Can you think of..."

"Crenshaw, what are you doing in the middle of my police investigation?"

A booming voice froze them in their seats for a brief moment, then Alex shot to his feet and confronted the newcomer. "Who the hell are you?" he growled, moving to stand in front of Julie.

Matt strode up the hill and eyed them accusingly. "A detective with the Victoria Police Department, and gee, let me guess, you would be Alexander Friedman, am I right?"

"So what?" Alex said belligerently. "I can talk to whoever I want to."

"Alex, it's okay. Matt's a good guy—most of the time." Julie patted his arm, touched that he'd tried to protect her. "His bark is worse than his bite."

"Try me," Matt growled.

"Oh, quit trying to intimidate the poor kid. He's been through enough," Julie said, rising to stand beside Alex. "What are you doing here, anyway?"

Matt crossed his arms and rocked back on his heels. "I don't know, *possibly* trying to catch up to my person of interest in a murder investigation. The question *you* haven't answered is how did you find him first?"

Julie smirked. "My superior research skills?"

Matt shook his head and sighed. "Not funny, Jules. You know I can't have you traipsing through my case. Connor would have my head if you end up in danger."

"What's he talking about?" Alex asked, turning his head to look at her. "Who's Connor?"

Julie flushed, not sure how to properly describe her and Connor's relationship to the teen.

"He's her boyfriend, and my partner." Matt saved her the trouble. "He doesn't like when she tries to get herself killed. He's funny that way."

Alex's brows rose. "You've gotten in trouble before?"

"You could say that," Matt said before Julie could answer. She traded glares with him instead.

"If you're done having a *tête-à-tête* over my love life, can we get on with things?" She waved the notepad in the air.

Matt snapped it out of her fingers and glanced down at her notes. "What's this?"

"Hey," she cried. "That's mine. Give it back."

"You heard the lady," Alex roared, stepping into Matt's personal space. "Give it back."

Julie gasped and made a grab for his arm. "Alex, it's okay. We argue like this all the time. He likes to annoy me."

Alex stopped and glanced between them. "That's just weird."

Matt chuckled. "She makes life interesting, that's for sure." He pointed to the words Julie had underlined. "Now, what's this about a security guy?"

"Alex says Emily Carter received notes at school like the ones Taylor found. He told her to take them to the UVic security office and see if they could help."

"UVic?" Matt repeated. "Emily Carter was sixteen. Why would she be at the university?"

"She aced her courses," Alex said, pride ringing in his voice. "She made early admission into some business classes at the university. That's how we met." The light left his eyes. "I should have been there to protect her."

Julie traded looks with Matt. "Do you know how long she'd been receiving those messages, Alex?"

"A couple of months, maybe? I'm not sure," he admitted.

"The security office," Matt mused. "I was just there yesterday going over tapes from the grounds." His eyes narrowed in concentration. "You don't suppose..."

A security technician. It made sense. He had access to private information, was likely a computer expert, and knew exactly where these kids walked to get home at night. Julie's heart began to race. She was onto something, she knew it.

"I have to go," she announced, turning to grab her bag.

"Oh, no you don't," Matt stated, hand near his badge so there was no doubt who was in charge. "Go home and wait. Connor will call as soon as we have any information. I mean it, Jules. Go home."

Dammit. This was her lead. She deserved to be there when they made their arrest. "Yeah, yeah, I'm going," she said. She just didn't mention where she was going. White lies don't count, right?

CHAPTER TWENTY

Matt called Connor for backup on his way to the university and then he called their IT guy, Bob.

"Hey, man, it's Matt Roy. Remember that burner we talked about the other day? Is there any chance you could trace it back to where it came from? I'm thinking maybe we could link our perp to a store's video surveillance and help with a positive ID."

"Already on it," Bob said, clicking keys in the background. "I started with your vic's cell phone and tracked it back to a cell tower, but by then your guy had turned on his airplane mode figuring it would block anyone from tracing him. What he didn't realize, is every phone operates under two systems, one that connects to cellular and the other interfaces with the consumer. Airplane mode may only disable some features, while the phone could be giving out a 'ping' notification to the cell tower and you wouldn't even know it."

"And..." Matt said impatiently. "How does this help me?"

JACQUIE BIGGAR

"Well, oh grumpy one, it means that with the use of a Stingray—also known as IMSI catchers—I was able to trick his phone into replying with his location and data that can be used to identify him. The day you called me, he was within a hundred feet of your victim's cell phone at 1300 hour.

"The video surveillance tapes I received came from two sources and are grainy. We're working to clear them up now, but I can tell you your guy wears a uniform and is most likely middle-aged, going by the way he walks. I'll have more within the next day, or so."

Matt slapped the steering wheel. "I knew it. Thanks, Bob. I owe you one."

"I think it's more like a case, but who's counting? Go get 'im, Detective."

He planned on doing his best to do just that. He called Connor back. "Are you close?"

"Ten minutes, give or take. Any idea who we're looking at?"

No, and that was a problem. If they went in and started questioning every guard working at the university, it could tip off their suspect, giving him a chance to disappear.

"Did you talk to Bob? He confirmed our perp was there the day we questioned Gina Davis. He was right in front of us and we missed it." Matt cursed and slammed on his brakes as the car in front of him slowed to let another vehicle join the flow from a side road. He snapped on his dash strobe lights and wheeled around the slow movers with a squeal of tires.

"Shit. The only guy that struck a weird chord with me was the one sitting near our table, did you notice him? He had a lisp but didn't look anything like the sketches Micah Miller sent."

He'd been too busy caring for the ill girl and frankly feeling sorry for himself to see who Connor had interviewed. But the lisp... that sounded familiar.

The security officer who'd helped him with the cameras had a lisp. Could it be...?

Son of a b—

"I know who the killer is. He must have worn a disguise, that's why I didn't recognize him sooner. Hurry, Connor, we can't let him get away." Matt clenched his jaw and sped across town. He could scarcely believe his sister's murderer had sat right beside him—he'd even shook the prick's hand.

He roared into the parking lot, cut his lights and slowed for the numerous students strolling across the pavement. He pulled up a couple of rows away from the security building and shut off his car. Urgency was a hunger eating at his insides. He needed in there—now.

He checked his sidearm, debating the wisdom of what he was about to do, and climbed out of the car. Connor couldn't be far behind. It wouldn't hurt to reconnoiter and get the lay of the land. The last time he'd been here, there'd only been the two guards on duty, but he'd like to be sure before they stormed the entrance.

Easing his way along the outer edge of the lot, he came up on the office from the rear and edged between the buildings until he was next to a window where he could peer inside. One guy, his back to Matt, sat at the computer station, a cup of coffee at his side. Where was...?

"Looking for someone, cop?"

The voice near his ear, sent shivers up Matt's spine, as did the weapon poking him between the shoulder blades. Slowly, he straightened. An ominous click halted any attempt to reach his sidearm.

"I don't want to shoot you here, but if you make me, I'll have no choice." The man shoved the barrel of his firearm deeper into Matt's back. "Now spread your arms real slow and don't move. I ain't playing games, I *will* put a bullet through your heart."

Left with little choice, Matt did as told and prayed no innocent bystanders would pay for his stupid mistake. He was frisked and relieved of his weapons and forced to his knees before his nemesis showed himself.

"Thought you was a smart one, did ya? I have news for you, *cop.* I've been doing this since you were damn near in diapers. It'll take more than the likes of some wet-behind-the-ears rookie to take me in." His brown eyes shone with an unholy light. He threw a set of cuffs at him. "Put them on and hurry up about it— I ain't got all day."

He'd changed his appearance again, but now that Matt knew who he was, he could see the resemblance from the drawings Micah had sent. The man's wig had become dislodged while he'd been tying Matt up, and it gave him the look of Moe Howard from the Three Stooges—though there was nothing funny about the situation.

"Look, turn yourself in and it'll go easier for you. Kill me and you'll have every cop in Canada gunning for you, your choice." Matt deliberately shifted to keep the gunman's focus on him until Connor could hopefully get into position to take him down. "Why the girls? Does it make you feel like a man to hurt those who are more vulnerable than you?"

"*Shut up*," Stanley spit out. "You have no idea what my life has been like."

Matt could see his nametag embroidered above his pocket—Stanley Webber. "Yeah, well, save your sob story for the courtroom, buddy. You're going to need it."

"We'll see," Stanley muttered, his lisp more pronounced. "Maybe I plan on going down in a blaze of glory, did you think of that, cop?" He wiped spittle from the corner of his mouth. "I could become infamous like Jack the Ripper or the Zodiac Killer. Yeah, I like that idea. They'll be chanting my name for years to come."

The guy wasn't running on all cylinders. How the hell was Matt supposed to get out of this mess?

He caught movement behind the psycho and hurried to keep his attention, meanwhile praying it wasn't a civilian. "You have a middle name, Stanley—if that's even your real name? Most infamous killers go by three names, makes them easier to remember, I guess."

Stanley glanced down at the nametag and smirked. "Did you think I only killed women? Dear old Stanley should have known better than to open his door to a stranger. Stranger danger, you know." He giggled like an idiot.

"Hey, dumbass, anyone ever tell you you laugh like a girl?" Julie yelled from behind them, a can of bear spray in her hands.

Stanley screamed as the stream hit his face, dropping the gun to cover his eyes, swearing like a muleskinner. He crashed to his knees, drool hanging from his mouth, and then flopped to the ground.

Julie edged around him, her eyes wide, and hurried to

Matt's side. "Oh, my God, are you okay? I saw him sneaking up on you, but I was too far away to help." She glanced over her shoulder. "Alex, call 911, hurry."

Matt couldn't believe Jules was here. "I thought I told you to go home. What the hell, Crenshaw? You could have been seriously injured."

She raised a delicate brow. "Pot, kettle. Do you want me to untie you, or leave you like this for your friends to see?"

Dammit, of course he didn't want them to see him like this. He struggled to his feet and turned slightly so she could work on the zip-cuffs. "My knife is on the ground over there." He pointed with his chin. "Cut them off, and for Pete's sake, get his gun. Hurry before that asshole comes to."

Julie kicked the gun into the bushes, then searched until she found the Leatherman and sawed at the plastic while Alex watched from the sidelines.

"Is that him?" he asked. "The guy who killed Emily?"

Matt nodded. "We got him, kid. You did good." He knew it was small compensation, his own feelings were all over the place, but his heart filled with relief it was finally over.

The ties bit into his wrists with the pressure Julie was applying. He glanced back and grimaced, muscles straining to split them apart. "Are you having fun back there?"

"Well, now that you—"

"Look out," Alex cried just as Stanley plowed into Matt's legs, sending him careening into the wall, pinning Julie with his weight.

"C'mon, cop, show me what you've got," Stanley snarled,

landing a solid blow to Matt's midsection as police sirens wailed in the distance.

Matt grunted from the force to his sternum and what felt like a dislocated kneecap. Clenching his jaw, he ripped the flexi-cuffs apart and used his palms to give his opponent a shot to the ears as though he was back in the school band playing symbols. Stanley dropped to the ground, his eyes rolling back in his head.

Julie groaned and pushed ineffectively against his back, but Matt couldn't afford to take his eyes off Stanley again. "Hang on, Jules. I have to take care of this cockroach, first." He glanced at Alex. "Thanks, man. You okay?"

Alex nodded, a big stick in his hands. "I'll kill him if he moves," he swore.

Matt reached for another set of plastic cuffs and reached down to yank Stanley to his feet. "I wouldn't piss the kid off if I were you," he murmured, snapping the cuffs on his wrists and then his feet. "He doesn't like you. Then again, none of us do."

Stanley just blinked at him through blurry, pain-filled eyes, the wig hanging over one ear. He was the sorriest looking killer Matt had seen in a long time.

Connor came in fast and low, gun in hand, with five other officers guarding his back. "Matt, you good?"

Matt gave a tired grin. "I'll be better when you read this creep his rights."

"Well, I'll be better when I can breathe," Julie growled from behind him.

Matt gave a startled laugh and turned Stanley over to an arresting officer before moving aside so Connor could sweep in and cuddle his woman.

Leaving them to a bit of privacy, Matt walked over to Alex. "Were you really going to bean him with that thing?" He nodded at the stick.

Alex stared after the officers loading Stanley in the back of a police cruiser, a circle of pedestrians watching the action. "Damn right," he said.

Well, okay then. Matt smiled and tugged the kid close. "I'm glad you're on my side," he said, and meant it. There was more than enough evil in the world, the good guys needed all the help they could get.

EPILOGUE

Matt thanked the cab driver and climbed out, his heart at peace for the first time since he'd begun these yearly visits. The grass was lush and green, a thick carpet running between the stately, and not so stately, gravestones. Some were plain, with little more than the deceased person's date of birth and death. But others had photos, heartbreaking pictures of little girls with curly hair and grandfathers with gentle eyes.

He had the location of Katrina's marker memorized and slowly made his way to her resting place. She'd loved nature, so he'd requested a plot near trees and now birds greeted him with their shrill songs as he set the bouquet of daisies near the base of the stone. Kat watched him, forever immortalized with her sweet smile.

"Well, I got him," Matt said. "I know, you told me to let it go, but I couldn't. Not without getting you the justice you deserve." He reached out and touched the granite. "I miss you, sis."

He called his stepmother, but she hadn't been able to bring herself to join him today. Losing her daughter had forever changed her life. His father was in the United States with his new family and had expressed his pride in Matt.

"I'd love to come, son, but you know how it is. Beth and the kids have plans for this weekend..."

Yeah, he understood. Some pain went too deep to face. It was easier to bury it deep and build new memories over the old.

"His name is Jeremy Daniels. He changed identities over the years like a chameleon. When we found him, he'd killed a new security guard at the University of Victoria. It gave him cover and an easy way to stalk his victims." Matt crouched and picked at a blade of grass. "I met someone, Kat. I think you'd like her. She's smart, sassy, and doesn't put up with my crap." He laughed. "She doesn't know I'm interested, but that's okay, I want to take it slow. My head hasn't been in the best place, so I think it's best if I take some time to... you know, settle after all of this."

He stared at her photo, her long dark hair and velvet brown eyes. She'd been as lovely inside as she was on the outside. That's how he planned on remembering her from this day forward. For so long, all he could picture was the pain and torment she'd endured, but with Daniel's arrest a weight had lifted.

He'd done his job.

Rising, he pressed a kiss to his fingers and placed them on her brow. "See you next year, kid. Love you forever."

Just as he was about to leave, a butterfly fluttered over the gravesite and landed on the headstone. Matt stilled, awed by the certainty his sister had sent the tiny creature as a sign of her love. A moment later, it lifted and flew toward the heavens in a ray of light and Matt felt all his lingering anger fall away.

It was time to live. And maybe, if he was lucky, love.

AFTERWORD

Reviews are the lifeblood of any successful author. Without you, we can't be heard. If you enjoy the story, please consider sharing on your favorite social media sites:

Please click here to post a review:

Amazon

BookBub

Goodreads

Thank you,

Jacquie Biggar

FREE DOWNLOAD

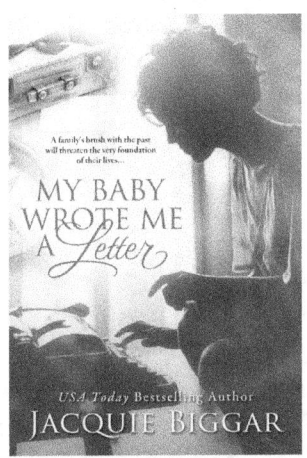

My Baby Wrote Me A Letter

A family's brush with the past will threaten the fabric of their lives.

Eight months pregnant and her Navy husband away on a mission, Grace Freeman craves the security of her childhood home in Canada.

When a letter written by her long-lost mother is found in an old writing desk it creates a tear in the fabric of her family.

Can Grace find a way to bring peace to those she loves, or will a message from the past destroy their future?

Newsletter subscribers also get bonus content and insider information every month. I love giveaways and there is lots of interesting stuff for me to share with you!

Newsletter- Sign up Now!

PREVIEW SKATING IN THIN ICE

Mac Wanowski was having the best night of his hockey career.

Two goals and three assists with a period and a half to go. Everything was going their way. He should be a shoo-in for MVP. The Victoria WarHawks were playing on home turf to a full stadium of rowdy fans with fast ice—nothing could stop him now.

The blow came out of nowhere.

One minute he was flying down the ice with the puck held in the sweet spot of his stick, the crowd roaring his name, the net in sight, in the next instant Mac was shoved from behind and smacked into the boards. He bounced and went down hard on his right knee. The pain was immediate and intense. It sucked the breath from his lungs and left him seeing stars. He dropped his head between his arms and tried to remain conscious until the medics arrived. It was small consolation the refs caught the illegal move and rang the penalty buzzer.

Fricking Murtagh.

The other team's enforcer liked to pull sneak attacks. He'd done it before. Mac rolled onto his back and blinked as the auditorium swam before his eyes.

"Wow, man, that had to hurt." Samson chortled, skidding to a stop against the boards. The plexi-glass shook with the collision.

Edwards, the team's doctor skated across the ice in his dress shoes and dropped to his side. "Hey, Hammer, nice hit. How you doing?"

"Been better," Mac grumbled. He squinted through the face-shield and yanked off his gloves. "It's the knee, Doc. Screwed it good this time." The helmet came next, clattering onto the ice along with his dreams.

"Don't worry. He will pay." Lazlo, the grinder, towered over Mac glaring at the other team as though daring them to come near.

"Keep it clean, boys," the ref said, gliding up to pat the Croatian's arm. "I don't wanna send you to the bench, but I will." He exchanged a look with the doc, then blew his whistle and waved an arm over his head. "Gurney's on the way."

Mac growled and tried to sit up, but Edwards forced him down. The guy might be old but working around a bunch of hockey players kept him in shape. "Take it easy, Mac. It's just a precaution. You don't want to aggravate that tendon any more than you need to."

Getting hauled off the ice like an invalid only added insult to injury. Not even the crowd's support could ease his wrath against the meathead who'd taken him down. He strained to see past the EMT's hold on the gurney. Murtagh sat in the penalty box, his arrogant gaze triumphant even as his coach tore him a new asshole from over his shoulder.

Pissed, Mac pointed and mouthed, "You're mine." Then they were in the hallway heading toward the dressing room and his adrenaline waned, leaving him drawn and listless. The knee throbbed, pressing uncomfortably against his protective padding. His shoulder ached from smashing into the wall and his insides jiggled like a bowl full of jelly. But if Doc gave him the go-ahead he could still make the third period. He needed to get out there and support his team, dammit.

Coach was waiting when he arrived, pacing and muttering while running a hand over his thinning pate. The second the

147

EMTs set him down on the exam table Coach was breathing in his face.

"What the hell, Wanowski? I told you to pass! This super-hero complex of yours is costing the team. Now what are we supposed to do, huh? We're already two men down and play-offs are coming up. Your actions tonight might have cost us the season. How do you feel now, asshole?"

Like shit, thanks for asking. The man had it in for him ever since Mac hooked up with his daughter for one never-to-be-repeated night, and nothing he did for the team was enough. It bothered him that this time Coach was right—he'd screwed up. Not that he could admit it, especially with all the interested ears wagging in the room. So, he said nothing.

The coach threw up his hands and stormed out of the room, heading back to what was left of the game. Mac just hoped they could retain their five-three lead until it ended.

"You like playing with fire, don't ya?" Doc Edwards shook his head. "Your contract is almost up with the WarHawks, Mac. Have you given any thought to what comes next?"

Mac frowned at the doc's back as he turned away to open his medical bag. "You hear something you want to tell me about?" He'd given three of his best years to this team. If the franchise planned to trade him off, the least they could do was tell him to his face.

Doc held up his hand. "Don't get your shorts in a knot, kid. I merely meant you can't play hockey forever. You must have a backup plan, right?'

Kid. Mac grunted as the other man loosened the ties on his knee guard. The resulting relief was quickly replaced by agony as blood rushed to the injury. He clenched his fists against the cool metal of the exam table and stared at the ceiling with its ugly track lighting while Doc poked and prodded the area like a sadist.

No, he didn't have a backup plan—this was it for him. Hockey was in his blood. It fed his dark soul and gave him the only true joy he'd ever known.

He couldn't leave the game.

"How bad, Doc?" He tipped his head to look down the length of his body and swore. Just as he'd thought, the knee was swollen and already showing signs of bruising. Last time he'd injured it, he'd ended up with water under the kneecap and had to have it drained. Fun times.

Edwards snapped an ice pack into action and set it against his skin before meeting his worried gaze. "I won't know for sure until we do x-rays. My best guess is your ACL." Mac winced. "Hopefully it's a sprain instead of a full tear which would mean surgery and months of rehab."

Christ, just what he didn't need right now. He laid down and covered his eyes with his forearm. "And if it's a sprain?"

"Sorry, Mac. You're still looking at two-to-four weeks recovery time, physio, and preferably crutches. I know someone, Sam Walters, who's good at this sort of injury. I'll call and see what I can get lined up."

Mac let him drone on with his voice of doom, meanwhile inside his stomach twisted into their own disastrous knots.

What was he going to do now?

Pick up your copy today!

ABOUT THE AUTHOR

Jacquie Biggar is a USA Today bestselling author of romance who loves to write about tough, alpha males and strong, contemporary women willing to show their men that true power comes from love. She lives on Vancouver Island with her husband and loves to hear from readers all over the world!

In her own words:

"My name is Jacquie Biggar. When I'm not acting like a total klutz I am a wife, mother of one, grandmother, and a butler to my calico cat.

My guilty pleasure are reality tv shows like Amazing Race and The Voice. I can be found every Monday night in my armchair plastered to the television laughing at Blake and Adam's shenanigans.

I love to hang at the beach with DH (darling hubby) taking pictures or reading romance novels (what else?).

I have a slight Tim Hortons obsession, enjoy gardening, everything pink and talking to my friends."

Subscribe to her Newsletter and follow her on these sites:

Amazon
Website
Facebook
Twitter
Google+
Goodreads
BookBub Page
Pinterest

ALSO BY JACQUIE BIGGAR

WOUNDED HEARTS SERIES

Tidal Falls

The Rebel's Redemption

Twilight's Encore

The Sheriff Meets His Match

Summer Lovin'

Wounded Hearts Box Set

Maggie's Revenge

With This Heart

MENDED SOULS SERIES

The Guardian

The Beast Within

Virtually Gone- High Tech Crime Solvers

GAMBLING HEARTS

Hold 'Em

Crazy Little Thing Called Love

My Girl

Married to The Texan- Box set

BLUE HAVEN

Sweetheart Cove

Sunset Beach

MEN OF WARHAWKS

Skating on Thin Ice

The Player

SINGLE TITLES

Silver Bells

The Lady Said No

My Baby Wrote Me A Letter

Tempted by Mr. Wrong

Valentine: A Hearts and Kisses Romance

Mistletoe Inn

The Sister Pact